BUTLER TO THE DARK LORD
A GRIM CHOICES GAMEBOOK

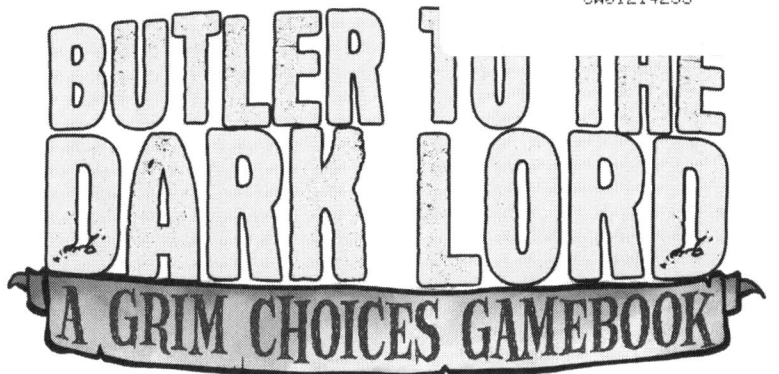

SAM BOWRING

Copyright © 2015 Sam Bowring

All rights reserved.

ISBN: 1512341045
ISBN-13: 978-1512341041

ABOUT THE AUTHOR

Sam Bowring is a writer and comedian living in Sydney, Australia.

www.sambowring.com

His other books are:

The Broken Well trilogy
Prophecy's Ruin
Destiny's Rift
Soul's Reckoning

The Strange Threads duology
The Legacy of Lord Regret
The Lord of Lies

Sam, Jake and Dylan Want Money
Black Market Prawns
The Summer of Our Discontent
Hell Freezes Over

For children 3+
The Little Bad Wolf
Sam the Cat

twitter.com/sammyfantastic
facebook.com/sambowringauthor

INTRODUCTION
by Stygias, the God of Shadows

Greetings, mortal scum. It is with small pleasure that I introduce to you this tale, a frivolous and passing fancy in which you play the main character. On the pages herein you will be offered choices – in stark comparison to your actual life – which will shape and bend the story to certain different ends. Perhaps you will die horribly along the way, or perhaps you will persist until the tedious finish. I don't care, really.

There is one key thing to keep in mind as you traverse the tale ahead. Whenever you see a word written in CAPITALS, that is what we shall call a 'note'. Notes let you access unique choices and open alternative pathways in the story. Write them down in the space provided, or if you possess intelligence greater than a miscarried goat foetus, you can remember them.

Notes can be good or bad. Don't feel pleased with yourself just because somebody SENT YOU SOME CAKE. It might be full of crow shit. Alternatively, HAVING LICE may seem like a misfortune, until you need to bribe a horde of ravenous baboons.

Neither of those things happen in the story, by the way. I'm just trying to hammer a simplistic example through your skull and frankly, I don't know why I bother.

Lastly, a word about cheating. Since you are evidently a person of low moral character, of course some cheating is expected. I will not try to ward you off it. A Great and Terrible God of Shadows like me does not give a roon's baloo about some dull-eyed bookworm sticking their thumb into a tome of questionable taste in order to keep their place while they scout ahead. That said, a word of advice – choose your moments well. Remember what I said about the cake.

And now, Mr Artanon, on with your tale.

NOTES

1

Well, Mr Artanon, look at you. Who would have thought that the son of a lowly spider farmer could rise to such esteemed heights? Yet here you are, standing in the kitchens of Cayfax Castle, dressed in the finest livery onyx can buy. For you, sir, are butler to Malacandros, Dark Lord of all Nocturnia.

The flames of fireplaces tickle suspended pots, which thicken the air with competing scents. Workers along stone benches busily chop and kill ingredients – nothing but the best for his lordship, of course. In the centre of the chamber a great oven blazes, its cracked chimney oozing smoke.

'Ah, Mr Artanon,' simpers Repugnis, the head cook. He's a fat goblin who samples too many of his own creations, as evidenced by his bulging belly and the delta of stains down his apron. 'I'm roasting his Horrendousness a prime briar beast basted in snake oil. Mmm-mmm! The intestines are stuffed with rotten apple and breadcrumb, and I've shoved a carrot up its arse.'

You arch an eyebrow, for Mal is already situated upstairs in the dining hall. With midday waning, he will be growing hungry.

'And just how long,' you ask, 'do you intend to keep his lordship staring at an empty plate?'

Repugnis titters nervously, and glances towards the oven. 'Good sir, a roast takes as long as a roast takes. If I stoke the flames any hotter the skin will crisp to charcoal. At best I could aim for a rare cut?'

What is your reply?

'It's you who'll get a rare cut across that corpulent neck of yours if you don't speed things along, you feckless blob of festering lard.'
Turn to 64.

'Surely in such an industrious kitchen, there must be a starter or two ready to send along and sate His Abhorentness's appetite?'
Turn to 91.

2

You wake to the pale light of Nocturnia seeping sluggishly through your window. It is a new day, and with it comes a new day's challenges.

You arise, wash, and head up to Mal's bedchamber. With his hated cousin due to arrive at any moment, Mal is insistent that he look his very best. He has decided that ceremonial armour, although somewhat impractical, will nevertheless project the right amount of 'imposingity'.

'This will only take a moment, Your Rank-and-Foulness,' you say, as you hang a necklace made from the bones of Mal's enemies around his neck – your careful way of asking him to stop twitching and let you do your job.

Soon enough the picture is complete; Mal wears a black cuirass carved with glaring eyes, his favourite helmet with the curled horns, and spaulders with spikes that stick out dangerously at eye level. He inspects himself in the mirror, turning this way and that.

'Does this culet make my behind look big?'

Do you reply:

'Your behind with well within the limitations of popular fashion, my lord.'
Turn to 146.

'Yes, my lord, your behind is an enormous blight upon the world, horrible beyond words.'
Turn to 120.

3

You awaken to the sound of lizard-birds screeching outside your window, heralding sunrise with their ear-piercing cries.
    The day of the ceremony has finally arrived.

Are you a NEGOTIATOR?
Turn to 54.

How about a BLACKMAILER?
Turn to 23.

If not ...
Turn to 7.

4

'Thank you, sir! Oh, thank you!'
    You have sworn to rescue Roseblossom.
    Your mind races as retrieve the booze cart and deliver it to the kitchens. Your very soul is on the line now, Mr Artanon – you have effectively ruined the Stygias Ceremony ahead of time, and only you

(and maybe the Shadow God himself) know it.

Running away does actually seem to be the best option.

What are you going to do?

Despite what you have promised Roseblossom, you could still abandon her to her fate, and try to work out some way to save your own skin in the meantime? In which case, go to bed and hope a new day brings a solution.
Turn to 96.

Or you could try to escape the castle with a beautiful (not to mention grateful) woman – not the worst thing, really?
Turn to 237.

5

You pass a row of cages containing ravens, most commonly used to send messages. Further on are some compartmentalised lizard-birds, hissing at each other through their bars, though what purpose they serve you are not sure. Live food for the wyrms, maybe? A shadow owl blinks at you, its dark eyes glimmering with unknowably owlish thoughts. A handler fusses over a pen of baby grimlings who can't yet fly – leathery little beasts with deep set eyes and spiny tails, which are hand-raised here before being allocated to scouts and hunters.

Interested as you may be in these creatures, the smell is growing quite overwhelming. It really is time you spoke to Molsk.

Turn to 118.

6

You enter a dry room with a low roof, in which row upon row of clothes hang from racks. A workbench covered with pins, needles, and strips of fabric is well lit by multiple hanging lanterns. Bojanda is very particular about the details of her work, as any good tailor should be.

'Miss Bojanda? Are you here?'

A rustling comes from the back of the room, and Bojanda emerges from between racks. She is a harpy – part humanoid and part bird – with wings folded across her back, and clawed hands which are precise and excellent for threadwork. Her crest is a mohawk of scarlet feathers, her beady eyes are blood-red, and her pendulous breasts hang uncovered from her bony ribcage.

'Ah, Mr Artanon,' she croaks, bobbing to the bench to lay out a robe she has retrieved. 'I'm about to start shortening the sleeves. His lordship will want to look sharp on his big night, eh?'

'I could not agree more, Miss Bojanda.'

'Had to dig around a bit to find this. Hasn't been a Stygias Ceremony for quite some time, eh?'

'About a hundred years, I believe.'

The robe is glossy black and gold-threaded with arcane symbols, and a patchy peppering of feathers sprout from each shoulder.

'Hmm,' says Bojanda. 'Seems we've lost a few there. Ah well.' She reaches up and plucks some feathers from her crest. 'One of the advantages of being a harpy tailor, eh? Heh.' She starts affixing her feathers to the robe. 'That'll do the trick. Lucky that I keep myself well groomed. It's a rarity, you know, for a harpy.'

'What's that, Miss Bojanda?'

'To be remotely concerned with appearance - or even hygiene for that matter. Honestly, back home in the roost, the girls fling their shit around like snowballs. Always did find it rather strange that the surest way to a harpy's heart is to compliment her smell. Guess that's why you don't see many men queuing up around the nests, eh?' She glances up. 'Is there something I can help you with, Mr Artanon?'

'Just making sure you're on track, Miss Bojanda.'

Everything here seems fine – Mal's ceremonial robe should be ready in plenty of time.

Turn to 124.

7

You head up to Mal's chambers to dress him magnificently for the day ahead.

'I tell you, Mr Artanon,' he says, as you put him in a svelte green jacket with spiky tassels dangling from the sleeves, 'I wish we could skip ahead to the evening. I have little appetite for breakfast, nor hobnobbing with treacherous nobility. The ceremony is so close at hand, I simply cannot concentrate on anything else. Hmm – do you think these tassels look silly?'

Do you say:

'They are terrifying tassels, lord, swinging from your elbows like the hanged villagers of sacked towns.'
Turn to 230.

'They are cheap and tawdry, lord, and will send your guests a clear message that you care little for their approval.'
Turn to 143.

8

'Need I remind you, Mrs Bleakheart,' you say, 'that should I wish it, I could have you lowered feet first into one of your own boiling vats?'

Bleakheart purses her lips thoughtfully. 'I believe I would thank you for that, Mr Artanon. Death would be a blessed relief in comparison to my workload.'

Staring into her dull, milky eyes, you decide you would much rather be elsewhere.

Turn to 124.

9

As the chanting grows louder, you glance around at the rapt faces of the crowd. You notice the werewolf groundskeeper Mr Feralis is staring upwards, his snarl curling and re-curling his lips as he tries to get himself under control. The moon, as low and powerful as it is tonight, is driving him bonkers.

'Mr Feralis,' you whisper.

He looks at you with wild, animal eyes. 'Mr ... Artanon ...' he manages. 'The ... moon ... calls. Can't ... keep ... clear. Need ... to ... rend and ... tear ...'

'You must maintain decorum,' you urge him insistently. 'Just a little while longer.'

'Can't ... hold ... on ...'

You can see he is near breaking point.

Are you a DIPLOMAT?
Turn to 116.

Or an INTIMIDATOR?
Turn to 50.

10

Beastmaster Jhurgle strides into the clearing holding a chain to the spiked collar of the beast that follows. She lopes like a heavy, muscular cat, her mane rustling in the breeze, her claws raking the grass to furrows, the moon reflecting in her huge black eyes. Handlers hold other chains and coordinate with each other as she swings her head this way and that to snap at the crowd.

'Set the beast before the altar!' commands Mal.

The handlers obey, forcing her into position and down onto her haunches while she growls angrily.

Jhurgle bows before Mal. 'We shall release her upon your word, oh Leader-like one.'

'Excellent,' says Mal. 'And now, my friends, I think this zagga deserves something to eat.'

The crowd titters in response.

'The virgin!' someone calls.

'The Brightlander bitch!'

'Let the zagga gnaw her bones!'

'Yes!' bellows Mal. 'Bring forth the virgin!'

A second group of priests appear, dragging between them a blonde Brightlander who weeps and struggles. They haul her to the altar and strap her down, while the restrained zagga watches on. She looks up and sees its slavering jaws, and shrieks in pure terror.

Mal steps forward to stroke her brow. 'You are right to be afraid, my darling.'

Have you DEFLOWERED THE VIRGIN?
Turn to 227.

If not ...
Turn to 180.

11

Due to a strange mishap of planning, there is no entry for poor old number eleven. So, why are you even reading this, Mr Artanon? Get back to work!

12

You're going to have to be pretty colourful to drum an impression into Molsk's stupid head.

Are you an INTIMIDATOR?
Turn to 167.

If not ...
Turn to 275.

13

Desperately, you turn to the crowd. 'Is there one of age among you who will step forth in offering? For the glory of your God, your lord and your land? Think of how you will be rewarded in the afterlife!'

'Actually,' says Mal, 'the afterlife isn't a very nice place for virgin sacrifices. I've spoken to the spirit of a former victim – she said she gets teased.'

No one seems eager to volunteer.

This isn't going very well, Mr Artanon. In fact, you can be assured that Mal is about to kill you in some horrible way.

Your service ends here.

14

You give the amber liquid a sniff and burn your nostril hairs off. You knock a dram back through your teeth, and grimace with pleasure. It's a strong whiskey, which warms you instantly. One for the drawing chamber, in moderate volumes, with plenty of ice.
 Next, will you try:

The *Graveyard Pearl* Black Sauvignon?
Turn to 197.

The Sparkling *Bloodworm's Rest* Cabernet?
Turn to 111.

Nargletarg's Vineyard Dry Blue?
Turn to 224.

Mrs Plugberry's Make-Me-Feel-Nice Cure-All Tonic and Tile Cleaner?
Turn to 87.

Or pile up a cart full of booze and get out of here?
Turn to 168.

15

You accompany the procession of food into the dining hall, which is met by much oohing and ahhing from guests. As sizzling, steaming, and squirming dishes are laid before them, greed springs into eyes as quickly as cutlery into hands. There is keen interest as the centrepiece is set down, for the large tureen swimming with balfrog tadpoles is expensive and exotic fare.

'My honoured guests,' says Mal, 'I invite you to eat with me this night!'

Several nobles freeze with forks already half-way to their mouths, and carefully put them down.

'On this hallowed occasion,' continues Mal, 'gorge of my larder and drink of my cellar, while you revel in your munificent and almighty lord - me!'

Sideways glances flicker about the table – this sentiment has no doubt been oft repeated during the speeches, and is perhaps growing tiresome. Still, the nobles nod dutifully and murmur their thanks.

'Now, feast!' says Mal.

There is a rush to the tadpoles and briar beasts, which Kalag and several others have a hard time carving up fast enough to meet demand.

Mal eases back in his chair and rubs his hands together as he considers the delicacies on offer.

'Ah, look!' he says gleefully. 'Conveniently placed just here, right next to me, it's my favourite food of all – peas!'

'Enjoy them, cousin,' says Nefarian. 'Tonight you deserve only the most spherical of vegetables. As for me, I shall sample some of this eel terrine. Do you know how long it's been since I enjoyed a mouthful of eel, cousin?'

'How long?' asks Mal, as he stuffs peas into his mouth.

'Longer than an eel!' chuckles Nefarian, cutting himself a liberal slice.

Well, Mr Artanon – as various folk around the table shove food into their gobholes, perhaps the time has come to check whether there's anything in particular we should be paying attention to?

If the BALFROGS ARE BAD ...
Turn to 214.

If the EEL IS DUBIOUS ...
Turn to 57.

If the PEAS WON'T PLEASE ...
Turn to 221.

If the FEAST IS FINE ...
Turn to 293.

If none of these things apply ...
Turn to 128.

16

As you open the door to Mrs Bleakheart's washroom, a thick cloud of steam engulfs you. You step inside, barely able to see a pace in front. Fires under iron pots stand out through the vapour, and the sounds of bustle come from all around as the silhouettes of maids move hither and thither.

Do you call out for Mrs Bleakheart to attend you?
Turn to 44.

Or go searching for her where the fires are brightest and thickest?
Turn to 105.

Or hug the wall and work your way around the chamber?
Turn to 27.

17

As you move about serving guests, Mal and Nefarian have a very public discussion.

'The skywatchers,' says Nefarian, 'have forecast a cloudless night tomorrow. Excellent conditions for the moon to shine.'

'Indeed,' says Mal, his flickering eyes the only holes in his mask of amicability. 'It is telling that such an extraordinary event occurs during my reign, wouldn't you agree? Evidently, I am favoured by Stygias.'

'Soon enough you will know for sure. To think that a mortal will speak to a god! Personally, I have no doubt that Stygias will grant you his approval - no doubt at all.'

You know, all too well, that Mal is worried about this particular aspect of the ceremony. History shows that, if the Shadow God is unhappy with the current ruler, he makes no bones about making them bones. While such executions are historically rare, they are undoubtedly a concern to any Dark Lord undertaking the ceremony.

Mal, however, hides his disquiet well.

'I am sure you are right, cousin,' he says with a smile.

Kalag appears by your side and whispers that lunch is ready to be served. You, in turn, let Mal know that he and his guests can move to the dining hall.

Turn to 213.

18

As they gnash away, Mal and Haiken discuss the Captain's recent raid on the town of Greenflower.

'Honestly,' says Haiken, 'those wretched Brightlanders are so easily slaughtered, sometimes I almost feel bad for them.'

Mal laughs at this hilarious joke. 'Ha! That's a good one, Captain. But tell me, what of your primary objective?'

'I am pleased to report success, my lord.'

'You have brought me a virgin?'

'She languishes in your dungeon even now – lovely, virtuous and ripe for sacrifice.'

'Excellent. My skywatchers predict a full moon in three nights time – perfect conditions for the ceremony.'

Footsteps sound at the dining hall entrance, and a goblin messenger, whom you recognise as Peedy, enters wearing a feathered hat and carrying a scroll.

Mal's gaze slides to him. 'What is it?'

Peedy clears his throat. 'Apologies for the interruption, Your Atrociousness. I bring you word from Vorganis Castle.'

'Oh?' Mal's tone is so instantly cold that the very temperature of the room seems to drop.

'Er ... yes, my lord. Lord Nefarian accepts your kind invitation to attend the Stygias Ceremony, and intends to arrive tomorrow morning.'

Mal's eyes narrow. You know he does not care for his cousin Nefarian, not least because the man is next in line to the throne. Nefarian's presence at the ceremony, however, must be tolerated, for he is a powerful lord in his own right, with many allies amongst Nocturnia's nobility – a fact which Mal does not enjoy being reminded of.

'Why bring me such news at lunch?' he growls. 'It has put a foul taste in my mouth and sullied my food.'

He drums his fingers on the dragon bone armrest, and fiery sparks flare at his fingertips.

Peedy quails, for he knows that Mal is prone to taking out his anger on the bearers of bad news.

It would be a shame, however (and a staffing issue), to lose a competent messenger to a moment of ill temper over something that really isn't his fault.

Do you attempt to intercede on Peedy's behalf?
Turn to 145.

Or abandon him to his miserable fate?
Turn to 71.

19

Repugnis calls for help getting another briar beast out of the oven, and the staff rally to him. While they are distracted you whisk out the jar and tap it out into the balfrog tureen. As the vicious little tadpoles churn about, they do a good job distributing the poison evenly throughout the entire dish, and dissolving it.

The BALFROGS ARE BAD.

Turn to 262.

20

You were pretty imprudent to give Roseblossom your real name, weren't you, Mr Artanon? Got swept up in the heat of the moment, did you?
　'It *is* true!' hisses Mal. 'I can see it in your face!'
　A weight presses down across your shoulders, like a heavy rope forcing you to your knees.

Are you a DIPLOMAT?
Turn to 278.

Or an INTIMIDATOR?
Turn to 157.

21

With a notable lack of reverence, you rip open the package and pull out the contents - a glass sphere and a parchment.
　Holding up the sphere, you see it is a snow globe, depicting the treacherous Narrowfang Mountains. Unrolling the parchment, you read:

SOOTHSAYING SNOW GLOBE
Shake the globe and know your future.

　You frown in distaste - you have seen such objects before. They are neither rare nor exotic, but rather an onyx a dozen from street-side merchants purporting to be dealers in magical goods, as opposed to tacky traders in gaudy nonsense.
　Still, if Ms Podger had received it a day or two earlier, perhaps she would have been told to 'Beware the Gravy'.

Do you want to:

Throw it in the trash and get on with other work?
Turn to 287.

Give it a vigorous shake?
Turn to 144.

Give it a gentle shake?
Turn to 225.

Give it a shake halfway between vigorous and gentle?
Turn to 60.

22

'You know, Miss Molsk,' you say, 'I have always found your feathers to be shiny and ... well structured.'

Molsk preens a little. 'Really?'

'Of course. And I'm certain others would enjoy their splendour too, if they weren't being constantly distracted by the stench of faeces in the air.'

Molsk appears not to catch your hint.

'If you like my feathers,' she says huskily, 'you're welcome to visit my nest tonight and help me pluck out the dead ones.'

Despite yourself, you cannot suppress the look of utter revulsion that Molsk's invitation brings to your face. Unfortunately she notices it right away, and her expression turns cold.

'Fine, then,' she says sourly.

Your attempt at flattery has reached a dead end.

Do you grab her by the neck and push her head into a pile of dung, to illustrate the disgusting state of the place?
Turn to 107.

Or, if you have really lost patience, why don't you reach for the dagger you keep about your person at all times, and stab her with it?
Turn to 93.

Or you could give up and leave?
Turn to 124.

23

A sharp rapping on the door sees you haul yourself from bed and go to the peephole. Rostolph and Nefarian wait outside. Wondering what you may have wrought, you open up and let them in.

'Forgive my lack of formal attire,' you say.

Nefarian smiles. 'I always find it interesting to see a servant out of livery. It's like when someone who wears spectacles takes them off - they look the same, yet different.'

Rostolph is more serious. 'You were wise, Mr Artanon, not involve Malacandros in your discoveries.'

'I hope so,' you say. 'I was wondering when I might hear from you.'

'Be assured,' says Nefarian, 'that I appreciate what a tyrant Malacandros can be, and I'm not speaking figuratively. Stick with me, Mr Artanon, and I can promise you rewards beyond your comprehension. Just a little insurance policy, before we continue ...'

Nefarian waves his hand, and a sinewy red

23 (cont'd)

thread springs into the air between you. It snakes into your chest, and you gasp as a warm knot ties itself around your heart.

'What ... have you done ... lord ...'

'A simple precaution, Mr Artanon. Your heart and mine are now linked. If mine stops beating, so will yours.'

Powerful magic indeed – Nefarian is as skilled a mage as everyone says.

You are BOUND TO NEFARIAN.

'So, you can see,' says Nefarian, 'it is now undoubtedly in your best interests that I succeed. Perform the task I give you, and I will undo the spell - not to mention shower you with riches.'

What else can you really say at this point?

'Very good, my lord.'

'We intend,' says Rostolph, 'to use the virulent poison you took on Malacandros at the ceremony feast. I have been trying to work out which dish would be best to secrete it in. Repugnis tells that Malacandros has a fondness for peas?'

'Indeed,' you say. 'He loves peas.'

Nefarian screws up his face in distaste. 'So, it's true. I mean, I knew he was evil, but not that evil. Yuck.'

'And you, Mr Artanon,' says Rostolph, 'will be in an excellent position to poison the peas just before they are served.'

'Then Malacandros dies,' says Nefarian, 'I become the Dark Lord, and a glorious new night falls over Nocturnia!'

'You take care of your part, Mr Artanon,' says Rostolph, 'and we'll take care of the rest.'

So, you are now a fully fledged traitor – but that is relative to who is in charge, eh?

Turn to 7.

24

'Ho, good sir,' you say, approaching the guard, who peers at you with piggy eyes from under his helm.

'Mr Butler,' he grunts.

'There's been a break out at the bestiary!' you say, trying to appear worried, which is not overly hard. 'All guards are too report immediately!'

The orc looks uncertain. 'I have strict orders from Captain Haiken not to leave my post. Only he can relieve me.'

'What are you talking about? Haiken is headed to the bestiary himself! Everyone is needed! Quickly, you must hurry, for a zagga roams free!'

The orc gives this a moment's thought, then shakes his blockish head. 'Sorry, Mr Butler, but it's not worth my hide. One more guard isn't going to tip the balance in a zagga hunt, and my instructions are very clear.'

There is nothing you can say to make this stalwart fellow budge, and he is wary enough now that you dare not attack him.

Frustrated and fearful, you retrieve your stashed bag and return to your room. It seems you must leave Roseblossom to languish in her cell, and try to figure a way to save your own skin.

It won't be tonight, however – go to bed, and try to get some sleep.

Turn to 3.

25

You hover by the briar beasts, looking for a good moment to sprinkle poison over one of them. For a moment the stars align and everyone has something else to do. You reach into your pocket and unscrew the top of the jar, then surreptitiously draw it out. As you raise your hand to the beast, someone bumps into you and the jar jolts from your fingers. It hits the floor and bounces away, the red powder spilling from it.

In annoyance you turn and find a squat goblin quivering behind a stick of bread clutched protectively to his chest.

'I'm ... s-sorry ... Mr ... Artanon ... I ... din ... s-see ...'

'Oh, just go away,' you say with a scowl.

As far as the food goes, the FEAST IS FINE.

Turn to 262.

26

'Ah, dear boy,' you say, lowering your voice to conspiratorial tones, 'do I detect some hint of fancy for that lovely young lady?'

Kalag blushes. 'I'm sorry, sir. I did not mean to be so obvious.'

You smile. 'I'll tell you what will be obvious, Kalag. If you don't do a faultless job cleaning his lordship's chair, I will have your belovéd's beautiful head mounted at the foot of your bed until such time as the flesh falls from her dimpled cheeks. That will be pretty obvious, don't you think, Kalag?'

Kalag turns very, very pale.

'Answer, boy.'
'Yes, sir. I apologise, sir.'
'So, what do you have to do?'
'The chair will shine, sir, you have my word.'
'Excellent.'

Satisfied that Kalag is sufficiently motivated, you may strike CHAIR IS DIRTY from your notes.

You leave the dining hall with TIME FOR TWO THINGS before needing to check in at your office.

Turn to 88.

27

You feel your way around the room with one hand on the wall, wondering if the steam and heat is giving your livery a good clean on the go.

You pass two figures stirring a pot with poles, and cannot help but overhear their hushed conversation.

'... can't believe she slept with Mr Rostolph, the undiscerning harlot!'

You recognise the voice of the chambermaid Jilly.

'I know,' says her friend. 'If Mrs Bleakheart ever finds out, she'll throw her in the hearth.'

Jilly scoffs. 'As if she'd know anything about it.'

'What do you mean?'

'Well, you know. She likes her sheets folded on the other side of the bed, if you take my meaning.'

'Um ...'

'She knows how to find a rat in a hole, if you catch my drift.'

'What?'

'She prefers the company of women, silly.'

'Oh! Really?'

'Rumour has it that the only man-orc who ever tried to touch her wound up with a broken wrist.'

'Ouch.'

You have learned BLEAKHEART'S PREFERENCES.

You continue on, and hear Bleakheart's voice coming from the middle of the washroom.

Turn to 105.

28

'It was Mr Rostolph!' Rose shouts.

A gasp goes up, and servants around Rostolph back away to leave him standing alone. You situate yourself amongst them, out of Roseblossom's view.

'What?' says Rostolph, aghast. 'My lord, I never ...'

'Is that him?' Mal asks, extending a finger towards Rostolph.

Roseblossom is desperate and confused, and you can almost see her make up her mind to lie.

'Yes! That's him! That ugly little bald man there, Mr Rostolph.'

Mal strides towards Rostolph, who looks like he's about to jump out of his skin - or be torn from it. Nefarian makes a hesitant move to intercede, but Mal's staff pulses, and he seems to think better of it.

Mal places the staff under Rostolph's chin and raises his head.

'Blood doesn't lie. Tell me, did you defile this girl? I suggest a yes or no answer - you might not have the heart for a longer one.'

Blood burbles from Rostolph's mouth. You've seen this spell before – the target can only speak the truth, though blood replaces breath.

'No!' Rostolph burps wetly with a spray of red mist.

Mal removes the staff, and Rostolph topples over.

'A lie,' says Mal, stalking back to the girl, 'designed to save your life. I commend your cunning, young woman, but it will not deliver you from the jaws of the zagga. Let the ceremony continue!'

Turn to 180.

29

But just because you are curious, does not mean you will find anything.

30

As a fireball builds at Mal's fingertips, you hastily clear your throat.

'Pardon my miserable intrusion, Your Violency,' you say, 'but the shortly forthcoming roast is infused with some unique and subtle flavours, which I fear may be overwhelmed by the stench of charred goblin. I would hate for this wretch to further contaminate your delicate palate, my lord.'

Mal glares at you, and for a moment you fear you have made yourself a new target ... but, after a moment, he waves his hand irritably, and the flames die out.

'Begone!' he shouts at Peedy, who bows and beats a swift retreat.

'This had better be one tasty briar beast, Mr Artanon,' Mal warns you darkly.

PEEDY LIVES, yet MAL IS IRKED with you.

Turn to 222.

31

'One moment more, I beg, my lord,' you say quickly.

'What now, Mr Artanon?'

You move closer to Mal and lower your voice. 'It occurs to me that, even though this harlot has falsely accused me, she may not be lying about absolutely everything.'

'You mean ...' Mal's brain begins to tick. '... some other man may have done the deed?'

'Who knows?' you say. 'It is a big risk to take, my lord.'

'You had best offer me an alternative or I'm just going to kill everyone and go home.'

'There is a servant no one would miss,' you say. 'And I know for a fact she has never laid down with a man. Use her instead, and be assured of her purity, technically speaking.'

'Well I did very much want to use a Brightlander,' Mal mutters in disappointment, 'but I suppose the rules don't expressly stipulate it. Who is this servant?'

'Mrs Bleakheart, lord.'

'Oh, *that* sour-faced harridan. I don't care for her at all.'

'She is quite loathsome, my lord.'

'She doesn't react to any of my threats.'

'Mine either, lord.'

'Come to think of it, I'll be glad to be rid of her.'

Turn to 254.

32

You lie back in the nice cold bath, enjoying the sight of your rubber duck-billed monster floating around.

33

You accompany Mal through the castle, flanked by Erkenslaw and his guards. Anyone you pass bows deeply, whether they be lowly rat herder or lofty noble. Those also on their way to the ceremony fall into step behind, until Mal leads quite the procession.

You leave the castle and make your way through the grounds to the ceremony plateau. A path through a wood emerges into a large clearing circled by obelisks. A crowd of nobles awaits, sparkling with jewels, fine armour and impractical weaponry. On the outer fringes servants and soldiers cluster, having been allowed respite from their duties to witness these momentous moments.

As Mal enters the clearing a cheer goes up, and shields and swords are shaken at the sky.

'Hail, the Dark Lord Malacandros!'

'Your shadow grows long and scary, lord!'

'Blessed by Stygias! Touched by the void!'

'Defiler of the Brightlands! Doom to all that's good!'

Mal chuckles. 'Quite the turn out, wouldn't you say, Mr Artanon?'

'I would, Your Self-Congratulatoryness.'

Mal waves to the crowd and heads towards the altar in the middle of the clearing, where gaunt priests in hooded robes scrape runes into the surface with mystical daggers.

As Mal passes Nefarian, he goes down on one knee. 'The stars are snuffed, my lord. The sky has emptied for the moon alone.'

Mal glances up at a moon that hangs unnaturally low, fat and yellow like a great eye, as if noticing it for the first time. 'Oh, yes. Will you look at that?' He smiles. 'Arise, cousin. I wouldn't want you to miss this.'

You take your place amongst the servants, on watch in case you are needed.

Mal reaches the altar. 'Welcome all!' he proclaims, his voice rippling through the crowd and silencing all chatter. 'You are here to witness a great moment in history. Once in a hundred years, a Dark Lord is chosen to offer sacrifice to the Great God of Shadows - the Eater of Light, the Swallower of Souls – and thus bestow his favour upon Nocturnia. Who is to be this chosen one, you ask, this champion of our land, this exalted conduit of fate? Why, it is I – Malacandros!'

Mal raises his hands, and another cheer resounds. You make sure that you clap politely.

'Bring forth the instrument of sacrifice!' calls Mal. 'Bring forth the fearsome zagga beast!'

Turn to 100.

34

As the chanting continues, an unearthly baying sounds in the woods nearby. It does not worry anyone much, as it fits the general atmosphere quite nicely.

There follows a breaking of twigs and a rabid snarl. A panicked feathertailed fox bursts from the tree line with Mr Feralis in hot pursuit, his eyes wild and froth streaming from his jaws. He bounds after his quarry through the crowd, knocking people to the ground. As the fox weaves through legs trying to find safety, Feralis swipes at it savagely with little regard for who comes between.

'What goes on?' demands Mal, of the growing

commotion.

'Mr Feralis!' you call, fearful for your friend. It seems you have chosen him prey that is simply too zippy!

The fox streaks towards the altar and Mr Feralis springs, claws flashing in the moonlight. He lands upon the fox and rolls, slashing the little animal to pieces. Highly prized fur and blood fly out around him.

'No!' shrieks Mal in horror.

A red streak spatters against the altar.

Turn to 284.

35

You nod to the guards and head back up the passageway. Carefully, so as not to break any bottles, you pull the cart up the stairs to the next level. There you walk past the dungeon door, and notice it is unguarded. You know the virgin to be sacrificed is being kept in there – would you like to take a peek at her?

Yes, indeed.
Turn to 104.

If you have been WARNED BY HAIKEN ...
Turn to 182.

No, because you are a responsible butler who keeps his mind on the job at all times.
Turn to 285.

36

Because everything has run so smoothly, make a note that you have TIME FOR TWO THINGS.

Turn to 88.

37

'I was taken by Mr Schazelburkus!' Rose shouts.

Mal turns slowly to the crowd, his eyes crinkling with amusement. 'Mr Schazelburkus, you say?'

'Yes! Yes!'

Mal laughs, and raises his hands in invitation to others to join him. They do, with genuine amusement.

'Why,' says Mal, 'I don't think anyone here goes by that name.'

'That's who he said he was,' Roseblossom weeps miserably.

'But, my dear,' says Mal, 'that name has not been in fashion since I wiped out the entire Schazelburkus family in order to take the throne!'

He roars laughter, and the crowd builds to a crescendo around him.

'Enough of these lies!' Mal bellows suddenly. 'On with the ceremony!'

Turn to 180.

38

Rostolph looks to you with questions in his eyes, and you shrug. You have poisoned everyone, it seems – but did you forget that your own life is now tied to Nefarian's?

Anger blazes in Nefarian's eyes as black veins stand out against his skin. You do not feel the pain yourself, thankfully – apparently, it's not that kind of voodoo. However, the moment that Nefarian gasps his last breath, death for you is instant.

'Mr Artanon!' yells Kalag urgently above the sound of a hall full of nobles shrieking and dying. 'What's happening? What are we going to do?'

He doesn't notice that your eyes have turned blank, even as you stand there. He does notice, however, when you crash to the ground.

Your service ends here.

39

'She is my whore,' you tell Feralis. 'You may not know this, but there are certain ... exotic ... choices one can make, if one speaks to the right person in the castle.'

'But Brightlanders?' says Feralis, wrinkling his snout.

'Not all of our noses are as sensitive as yours, Mr Feralis. While she no doubt smells repugnant to you, to a nasally challenged human like myself, the sight of flesh is next to universal. And men in positions of import like us must find ways to relieve our tensions. Hence I am looking for a secluded spot to spend some time with my purchase. I thought this patch of wood to be unpopulated, but sadly ...'

'Don't let me stand in your way, Mr Artanon,' says Feralis. 'I had no idea you were ... well ...'

'I am sorry to have brought you into it, Mr Feralis.'

'I shall see you are not disturbed,' Feralis says with a hint of disgust, and slinks away.

'Come,' you tell Roseblossom.

Turn to 193.

40

In the kitchen a couple of scullions scrub pots in the corner, while Repugnis dozes on a stool with his horny feet up on a food preparation area. As you clear your throat, his eyes snap open and he hastily rises.

'Mr Artanon,' he says. 'I wasn't expecting you so late.'

'I'm after a bite before bed,' you say. 'Ill-advised as that may be.'

'Of course, sir. What can I get you?'

Would you like some cheese?
Turn to 148.

Or some spikeberries?
Turn to 76.

Or dried strips of meat?
Turn to 203.

41

To your dismay, you notice that the idiot you entrusted with cleaning of Mal's dragonbone chair has failed to do their job properly! There is a still a ruddy great stain along the armrest, and from the expression on Mal's face, it has not escaped his attention either. He beckons you to him.

If MAL IS IRKED with you ...
Turn to 125.

If not ...
Turn to 152.

42

It is time for the next stage of the ceremony.
　'Release the zagga!' Mal cries. 'May it satisfy the endless greed of the great and terrible God of Shadows!'
　The zagga strains against its handlers, working itself into a frenzy. Jhurgle claps his hands, and they let the chains fall.
　The zagga springs at the terrified woman on the altar.

Is it a RED AND GREEN ZAGGA?
Turn to 246.

Or a BLACK AND YELLOW ZAGGA?
Turn to 147.

43

Perhaps it's time to make some kind of move! You know there is a jar of poison in Rostolph's quarters which he intends to slip to Mal somehow during the ceremony feast tomorrow night. Do you wish to utilise dinner time, when all lords and ladies will be in the dining hall attended to by their servants, assumedly including Rostolph, to take action?

Yes, it is time to strike!
Turn to 216.

You are optimistic you can find a better time!
Turn to 265.

44

'Mrs Bleakheart!' you call out. 'I require a word, madam!'

A few moments later, the orc housekeeper stalks towards you through the swirling mists, muttering to herself in annoyance. Her apron is patchy with moisture, and her thick brow drips condensation as she furrows it in your direction.

'Mr Artanon,' she says. 'You have an unenviable talent of interrupting me at my busiest.'

'I simply want to make sure you have everything you need. With so many guests arriving, I have trails of footmen marching about like ants to a kill.'

'Indeed,' she replies. 'Perhaps you can extrapolate from your own experiences then, and deduce I have my work cut out for me readying all the guest rooms?'

Are you a DIPLOMAT?
Turn to 166.

Or an INTIMIDATOR?
Turn to 236.

45

Feeling dangerous, Mr Artanon?

You move past Mal to Captain Haiken and, using a pair of tongs fashioned to look like crow's claws, start placing rat heads onto his plate. As you do, you glance surreptitiously at Mal, wondering if you have irritated him by serving his guest first – he is not exactly known for his good manners – but he does not seem to have noticed. At any rate, your first footman, Kalag – a young man who shows much promise – hops to action, to lay slivers of slug meat on Mal's plate.

'Er ...' says Haiken, his meaty hand skimming the tableware. You realise he is uncertain about what, amongst the array of cutlery laid out on either side of his plate, is the correct implement to use for rat heads.

Are you a DIPLOMAT?
Turn to 251.

If not, do you simply inform him which is the proper rat-head-eating-fork?
Turn to 95.

Or do you let him flounder?
Turn to 194.

46

When will you learn not to eat cheese before bed, Mr Artanon? You aren't as alert and clear-headed as usual. Hence, when you hear the sound of someone approaching, they are already too close for you to hide. Instead you stand up quickly and stride along the corridor towards whomever approaches, in what you hope is a very I-was-merely-walking-along-here-on-my-way-to-somewhere-else kind of manner.

Lord Nefarian appears around a corner ahead, appearing deep in thought. As you draw nearer, he notices you.

Are you IN NEFARIAN'S DEBT and BONDED WITH ROSTOLPH?
Turn to 158.

Otherwise ...
Turn to 102.

47

You have become OVERLY CURIOUS, Mr Artanon.

Turn to 29.

48

'Why,' observes Nefarian, 'the funk in here is very mild, for a castle aviary. My commendations to your staff, my lord.'

You stand a little straighter, knowing the hand you had to play in keeping Mal safe from potential insult, even though he remains none the wiser.

Turn to 66.

49

You return to the clearing and the impatient Malacandros.

'What news, Mr Artanon?' he asks through clenched teeth.

'There has been a ... technical hitch, lord. Everything will be rectified as swiftly as possible.'

'This has put slight dint in my momentum, would you not agree, sir?'

'Jhurgle assures me a beast is forthcoming, lord.'

'Did I not put you in charge of overseeing *everything*?' says Mal.

If MAL IS IRKED with you ...
Turn to 174.

If not ...
Turn to 218.

50

What will you say to shake some sense into Feralis?

'Don't force me to affix some kind of conical device around your head to make you behave, Mr Feralis.'
Turn to 97.

'If you interrupt the ceremony, Mr Feralis, I shall put you down like the dog you are.'
Turn to 215.

51

You make your way down to the grand entrance, and nod at armoured guards as you pass through.

The castle grounds are built all over the different plateaus of Cayfax Mountain. Paths run off in many directions through well-tended gardens of sculpted hedges, creeping vines, and weeping flowers. You make your way up a set of steps to a higher level, where you see a croquet course set up upon the grass. Nearby the groundskeeper's cottage lies nestled amongst willows, outside of which Feralis stands at a table hammering a shovel back into shape. He is a shaggy werewolf dressed in green overalls, whom you have never seen in human form.

'Greetings, Mr Feralis.' You nod at the shovel. 'A bit bent out of shape?'

'Hello, Mr Artanon – and yes, I had cause to clout a young orcling over the head with it, as he was trying to make off with some of his lordship's tomatoes. To what do I owe the pleasure, sir?'

Would you like to take a look at the front gate, through which some of the guests will soon be arriving?
Turn to 267.

Or inspect the site where the Stygias Ceremony will take place?
Turn to 240.

Or ask what the croquet set is all about?
Turn to 151.

52

You arrive at Nefarian's designated chamber, which has adjoining quarters for Rostolph.

'Here you are, Mr Rostolph. You'll find bells within if you need to summon servants. I trust you'll enjoy your stay with us here at Cayfax Castle.'

'Much obliged, Mr Artanon.'

You hold the door open for Rostolph, then hasten off towards the kitchens. Mal is still waiting for his wine and cheese!

Turn to 181.

53

You cannot help but feel a little sorry for Roseblossom as she gets eaten alive. Still, that isn't your greatest concern.

The zagga spits out what remains of Roseblossom's half-chewed body, and runs the back of her paw across her tongue in disgust.

'What ...' says Mal. 'Do you not enjoy the taste of unsullied flesh, beast?'

In the sky, the skull moans, and breaks apart into threads of cloud.

Mal is confused. You, meanwhile, get a sinking feeling in your stomach. Very, very sinking.

'Is ...' Mal looks at the sky uncertainly. 'Is that to your liking, oh Horrendous God? Her virgin blood has touched the altar! No matter that the beast finds her unappealing. The ceremony ... is complete?'

The skull begins to reform.

You edge towards the back of the crowd. Maybe it's not too late to run?

Turn to 284.

54

As you lie in bed thinking about the tasks ahead, you notice a funny sensation in your fingertips. Holding them up, you see that they are blackening. A searing pain accompanies the sight, and a moment later, your fingers are on fire!

An ethereal voice echoes about the room.

'You're probably wondering what is happening,' it says, and you recognise Nefarian. 'I've cast a little spell that locks onto the fingerprints you left on your letter, whoever-you-are. Honestly, did you think some tutor-like slap on the wrist was really going to foil my plans? You have made a rather unassertive choice, my friend, and now you pay the price.'

You scream as the flames spread, setting fire to the sheets. You tumble from the bed and tip a jug of drinking water over yourself, but it does no good – this fire is set underneath your skin.

Your service is at an end.

55

'My word,' you say, 'I just caught a whiff of you, Miss Molsk - like a mix of rancid sweat and decomposing meat. Most tantalising.'

Molsk turns bright red. 'Why, thank you, Mr Artanon. You certainly know how to make a girl feel special.'

'Mm,' you reply absently. 'Still, it's gone now. A shame I only caught it for a moment.'

Molsk looks worried, and wafts air from her armpits up towards her face to reassure herself.

You glance around casually. 'I'm sure your individual scent would be easier to pinpoint if it wasn't being muddied by all the competition.'

'Sir?'

'Well, amongst the wyrm turds and raven splatter, you really don't stand much chance, do you? You're just one of the crowd. On the other hand, if someone was to really scrape and scour the place, well, you'd stand out like a fart in a strawberry patch, wouldn't you?'

Molsk nods thoughtfully. 'I see what you mean, sir.'

'Indeed. Strip all rival odour from the chamber, and you would assuredly make yourself the apple of everyone's ... nose.'

Molsk turns excitedly to her workers. 'All right, you lot! Fetch buckets and water and, er, what do you call it, Mr Artanon?'

'Soap.'

'Yes, that's it - soap! Fetch all that and prepare for a cleaning frenzy!'

You allow yourself a moment to relish the surprise on the worker's faces before you depart from the chamber. It is safe to assume that the AVIARY IS CLEAN.

Turn to 124.

56

'Good evening to you, Captain Haiken.'

Haiken furrows his orcish brow, evidently trying to place you.

'Ah,' he says. 'You are Lord Malacandros' first footman, yes?'

'Butler, actually.'

'Hmm. I suppose household hierarchies are as

unfamiliar to me as soldier's rankings are to you. What is your business here?'

'Hmm? Oh, I ate a lot of cheese just before bed. It was a poor choice, indicative of a complete lack of common sense. I was just going into the dungeon to take in the calming atmosphere.'

'I'm afraid the dungeon is off limits at the moment, sir.'

The look in Haiken's eyes make you suspect there is little wiggle room in his stance.

'Well,' you say, 'I should probably try to get some sleep anyway.'

You traipse back to your bedchamber and eventually fall into a fitful slumber, in which you dream of trekking through a bizarre yellow landscape studded with triangular mountains full of holes.

Turn to 2.

57

Servants move in an endless train, clearing tables and bringing fresh plates. All is jolly and well. The exceptions are Nefarian and Rostolph, who you observe glancing from Mal's peas to Mal, first with an air of anticipation, then with growing confusion, and then, as time goes on, consternation.

Suddenly Mal coughs and pats his chest, and they immediately perk up.

'Feeling all right, my lord?' Nefarian asks with a devilish smile.

'Quite a lot of paprika on these peas,' observes Mal. 'Not a very traditional combination, but I do admire the cook's inventiveness.'

Nefarian frowns.

'More eel terrine, my lord?' you ask, bending over his shoulder to cut him a slice.

'Ah ... yes, thank you, Mr Artanon.'

You serve him and step back next to Rostolph.

'I can serve my own lord, thank you very much,' Rostolph says snippily.

'Don't get your shit-stained loincloth in a bunch,' you say with a sneer.

Rostolph is outraged ... but is instantly distracted as Nefarian lurches upwards from his seat, clutching at his chest.

'Everything all right, cousin?' asks Mal.

'Er ... just ... a little indigestion ...'

Frantically Nefarian daubs his mouth with a napkin, where froth bubbles at the corners of his lips. Sweating profusely, he loosens his collar, and reveals veins standing out blackly against his skin.

'What's going on?' demands Mal. 'Cousin, is this some of joke? Are you trying to ruin my celebration?'

Nefarian gestures at his chest. 'Poison ...' he gasps. 'Save ... me ...'

'Poison!' exclaims Mal.

Are you BOUND TO NEFARIAN?
Turn to 298.

If not ...
Turn to 239.

58

As you help Mal into his evening robe for dinner – a fashionable number with blue stars stitched on the chest – you sense he is still in a bad mood over his cousin Nefarian's impending arrival.

'Always he has coveted my throne,' he spits, and you subtly wipe the flecks from his sleeve. 'Even in childhood, he would attempt to befriend me or bring me nice presents on my Cursed-with-the-Blight-of-Existence Day. As if I could not see through the falsity of his gestures! Why can't he understand that I am the one born to rule, and he to crawling about in the mud with the worms and scuttlefangs?'

'Some people simply lack the grace to accept their station in life, my lord.'

'Keep a close watch on him while he's here, and report all findings back to me. Especially anything to do with ulterior motives, cunning plots or treasonous undertakings.'

'Of course, Your Suspiciousness.'

Once Mal is dressed, you accompany him down to the dining hall.

Upon entering, you note that some of Nocturnia's nobility have already arrived.

Have you TRUSTED IN OTHERS?
Turn to 41.

Otherwise ...
Turn to 75.

59

'There are plenty of virgins here,' you say, and point out a young brother and sister as an example. Their mother looks aghast, and hugs her children close.

'Won't work, Mr Artanon,' says Mal. 'If Stygias wanted children, he would have asked for them. He asked for virgins, and we all know that virgins,' he thumbs at Roseblossom, 'look like that.'

This isn't going very well, Mr Artanon. In fact, you can be assured that Mal is about to kill you in some horrible way.

Your service ends here.

60

Despite your misgivings, you give a globe a moderate shake and stare into its depths.

The snow swirls and forms into words, which sparkle and glow:

*Ultimate rule is within your grasp
if you think inside the circle.*

You stare at the words for a moment in horror, then quickly smash the globe on the ground. If Mal saw an underling reading anything of this nature, it would not matter if the words were carved in stone or shaved into a donkey's backside - that underling would be as good as gutted.

'Everything all right, Mr Artanon?' asks Sarka, poking her head in the door.

'Yes, yes,' you say, covering anxiety with irritation. 'Just send someone in to clean up this mess.'

Discover the future in your own time, Mr Artanon. *Turn to 92.*

61

You leave the kitchen to see Rostolph turning a corner ahead, and glide silently after him. He goes up a spiral staircase, and you pause to listen at the bottom. You know the castle inside and out, so you are able to tell by sound alone which way he heads once he reaches the top. You ascend and slip into a shadowy alcove.

Down the corridor, Rostolph cups a hand to his mouth and spits a tadpole – still alive and wriggling – into a handkerchief. No wonder his eyes were watering! Such an angry morsel would have torn the inside of his cheek to ribbons. But why in all Nocturnia would he want to smuggle a live balfrog out of the kitchen?

With your interest piqued, you follow him undetected back to his quarters, where he quickly shuts the door behind him.

You glance around – the corridor seems deserted.

Do you want to chance a glimpse through the keyhole into Rostolph's quarters?
Turn to 204.

Or you could knock on the door?
Turn to 122.

Or leave these strange goings-on and return to your office?
Turn to 142.

62

'His name is Mr Artanon!' Rose screams.

A gasp goes up around you, and all fall back to leave you standing alone. Slowly, Malacandros turns.

'Is that him?' he asks, extending a finger.

Roseblossom's maddened eyes meet yours.

'Yes, that's the filthy defiler! That's him right there, hiding in his fancy coat and polished shoes!'

'Mr Artanon,' says Mal. 'Is this true?'

Do you imagine you are about to have a moment of brilliance and somehow talk your way out of this?
Turn to 199.

Or do you think this is all going to end pretty badly for you?
Turn to 20.

63

'This has been an entirely disappointing day, Mr Artanon,' says Mal, acid dripping from his tongue.

You realise there is little hope for you now. You have failed twice in quick succession, and have seen more important people than you set aflame for less.

'Er ...' says Nefarian, but Mal's expression halts him, and he wisely decides not to interject this time.

Guests gasp as invisible forces seize your body and, with a wave from Mal, you are hurled off your feet to smash through a window. As you hurtle downwards, you're not certain if your sudden faintness is due to the rushing air or a loss of blood, but are at least fairly certain that it doesn't really matter.

The ground beckons.

Your service is at an end.

64

Repugnis turns a paler shade of green, and gulps.

'I beg you, Mr Artanon, stay your hand. I'm sure that something must be ready.'

The cook glances around and spots a bench at which several trays are being assembled.

'Ah!' he says. 'How about some pickled rat heads and carpaccio of slug?'

You scowl, long enough to make Repugnis quiver, then turn and snap at some lurking footmen.

'Get those trays up to his lordship without delay!'

The footmen spring into action, seizing the trays and heading for the door.

'Thank you, sir,' says Repugnis. 'The roast will not be far behind, I promise.'

'See that it isn't,' you reply, 'or the next item on the menu might be goblin stew.'

It seems you are an INTIMIDATOR.

Turn to 200.

65

Your lack of faith in your underlings drives you to do the job yourself. Stygias knows how Mal would react if forced to sit in a soiled seat! You send for bleach and washcloths, then set about scrubbing until the chair is spotless once again. Perhaps this task was technically beneath you, but at least you can remove CHAIR IS DIRTY from your notes.

You now have TIME FOR ONE THING before you need to check in at your office.

Turn to 88.

66

'Come, cousin,' Mal says to Nefarian, 'let us repair to the throne room, where you can dazzle me with stories of whatever-nonsense-you've-been-up-to.'

'Sounds delightful.'

'Mr Artanon, see that we are brought some wine and cheese.'

'Yes, my lord.'

You are about to follow them out of the aviary when somebody clears their throat behind you. You turn to find Nefarian's butler standing there with his master's bags draped all over him.

'Greetings, sir,' he whines. 'Allow me to introduce myself - I am Rostolph, butler to Lord Nefarian.'

'Ah, yes,' you say. 'Pleased to make your acquaintance, Mr Rostolph. I would shake your hand, but you seem somewhat encumbered.'

You pointedly eye his knuckles whitening on bag straps without offering to take one for him.

'No need for such pleasantries, sir,' says Rostolph. 'Though I wonder if you'd be so kind as to show me to my lord's appointed quarters?'

You really should attend to Mal's cheese desires immediately but, on the other hand, this could be a valuable opportunity to suss out this Rostolph character.

Will you personally show Rostolph to Nefarian's quarters?
Turn to 219.

Or do you call for Kalag, who is lurking nearby, and have him show Rostolph the way?
Turn to 127.

67

You approach the bushes and clear your throat. 'Is someone there?'

Feralis, the werewolf groundskeeper, pokes his head out. He looks unkempt and rather unhappy.

'Mr Artanon,' he says, plucking a bur from his cheek. 'Apologies, I did not see you there. On the other hand, I was trying to be sneaky.'

'Why so, Mr Feralis?'

Feralis glances up at the sky, where the moon is plump, if not quite full.

Have you already spoken with Feralis about the forthcoming full moon?
Turn to 119.

Or not?
Turn to 98.

68

Truth be told, you've found Mal a bit arduous to deal with of late. If others are out to kill him, you don't see any reason why you should stand in their way – as long as you stand to benefit from his demise!

You take out your notebook and pen a note which you hope to leave in the poison's place.

You are a BLACKMAILER.

Turn to 235.

69

You walk to the doors and look out over a scenic morass of briar and swampland, dotted by villages on the higher lumps. Directly below you are the castle grounds, built on the different levels of Cayfax Mountain. Oddly carved hedges stand along garden pathways, and soldiers train in sectioned fields or archery ranges.

One particular area catches your eye, out the back of the bestiary. A couple of handlers in the exercise pit are trying to get two zagga beasts under control, while a beggar child watches on from seats in the viewing area above. Pulling hard on the chains of the smaller black and yellow beast, the handlers manage to dodge its snapping jaws and haul it through a portcullis gate into darkness. The remaining beast, which is red and green, is left alone for a moment. It cocks its head thoughtfully at the child, then swings its long tail up out of the pit and manages to whack the viewing seats. The child tumbles forward into the pit, where the beast waits with open jaws. A couple of gulps later and the child is gone, with no evidence of his passing. The handlers return, none the wiser to what has just happened.

Shrugging, you turn away.

It is probably time you got on with things, and spoke to Molsk.

Turn to 118.

70

As revelry continues in the drawing chamber, you notice that Mal is sipping rather lightly on his drink. This is quite unusual behaviour, but perhaps he wishes to remain clear-headed for tomorrow's monumental proceedings? That said, he smiles or scowls whenever appropriate, and does a good job entertaining his guests, for a malevolent psychopath.

Finally the night winds down, and you are left to your own devices. You have noted during the course of the evening that booze supplies are running low, so perhaps it's time you visited the cellar to select more bottles to put into circulation?

However, if you are a BEDTIME RAIDER, you may have more important things to attend to?
Turn to 192.

Or perhaps you are a DELEGATOR who needs to meet with someone?
Turn to 217.

If neither of these things apply, you could go down to the cellar?
Turn to 277.

Or send Kalag to do it, and get some much-needed rest for the big day ahead?
Turn to 96.

71

'Oh, Displeaséd One,' stammers Peedy, 'I beg your forgiveness. I merely thought you would want to know ...'

With a snarl Mal shoots a hand forth to blaze a fireball along the length of the table. It hits the wide-eyed messenger directly in the chest, and Peedy barely has time to squeak before his body is engulfed in flames. His flesh melts away to leave behind a charred skeleton still wearing a jaunty hat.

'Bah,' says Mal, wiping his sooty fingers on the dragon bone armrest.

If it was not already, the CHAIR IS DIRTY.

Turn to 222.

72

You traipse back to your bed and eventually fall into a fitful slumber, in which you dream of trekking through a bizarre yellow landscape studded with triangular mountains full of holes.

Turn to 2.

73

You have already taken measures to satisfy Feralis, and really, he is the more important of the two. There is enough on your plate without taking on the troubles of every last staff member.

Give Sarka an encouraging scratch behind the ears and then head back to your office.

Turn to 211.

74

While everyone bustles about readying for dinner, you instruct Kalag to send for Jilly the chambermaid. When she arrives, you guide her to a less hectic corner.

'Mr Artanon?'

'Keep your voice down, girl. Now listen, I have a task for you of the utmost importance. Success will assure you a higher pay grade, but you must not speak to anyone about it. Do you understand?'

'Yes, sir.'

'Very well. I want you to make up the quarters of Lord Nefarian and his butler Rostolph while they are at dinner. Here's the tricky part – when you do, I want you to put some some bedbugs *back* into their beds.'

Jilly starts to look very worried.

'Sir?'

'Trust me, my girl, it's for the good of the castle. In days to come, I will explain everything. Can I rely on you?'

'Won't I get into trouble, sir?'

'I swear that not only will you not get into any trouble, you will be handsomely rewarded. Come, Jilly - you know me to be a man of my word, yes?'

Jilly bites her lip, but nods. It seems you have won her over.

'Now, be swift.'

She retreats to go and fetch some bedbugs.

You are now a BEDTIME RAIDER.

Turn to 265.

75

With important dignitaries in attendance, you watch your staff like a hawkbear. Thankfully they do you proud, and dinner goes by without a hitch. Afterwards, Mal and his guests retire to the drawing chamber for brandy and cigars, until Mal is sozzled enough to declare it bedtime.

As nobles stumble towards their rooms, you yawn and wonder if there is anything else worth attending to.

Will you go to bed and get a good night's rest?
Turn to 261.

If you're feeling peckish, you could visit Repugnis in the kitchen?
Turn to 40.

Or take a stroll in the castle gardens?
Turn to 129.

76

You eat a few spikeberries, and enjoy the sensation of their brittle casings popping between your teeth, to release puffs of dry, acrid soot that quickly coat the inside of your mouth. Mmm-mmm!

Now, enough fooling about! You have a big day tomorrow. Get to your bed chamber.

Turn to 261.

77

'Miss Molsk ... it is *Miss*, isn't it?'

'Er ... yes, sir.'

'Well, Miss Molsk, I wonder if anyone has ever told you that your pupils are bloodier than a well full of murdered Brightlander babies?'

'Oh my, Mr Artanon. No, they have not.'

'It's a shame that, reflected in their gaze, the dilapidated state of the aviary dulls their pulchritude.'

Molsk blinks her blank and hideously watery eyes at you. 'Huh?'

It seems you have wasted your flair for verbosity upon this slack-jawed dullard – time to try something else, Mr Artanon.

Do you grab Molsk by the neck and push her head into a pile of dung?
Turn to 107.

Or, if you have really lost patience, why don't you reach for the dagger you keep about your person at all times, and stab her with it?
Turn to 93.

Or you could give up and leave?
Turn to 124.

78

You stash your bag in an alcove and approach the dungeon door. To your dismay, an orc guard now stands watch. As you approach, you wonder how to get past him – or rather, how to get rid of him entirely, since you hope to be leaving the dungeon with Roseblossom in tow!

Are you an INTIMIDATOR?
Turn to 139.

If not, will you try to convince the guard to enter the dungeon with you, so you can finish him off inside?
Turn to 256.

Or will you pretend there's an emergency elsewhere that requires his attention?
Turn to 24.

79

With your hand tight around the jar of poison in your pocket, you survey the food. If you were going to use it, now would be the time. Despite the busyness around you, you are sure you can find a good moment to sprinkle some of the noxious stuff into a dish of your choice.

The question is, which one?

The balfrog tadpoles?
Turn to 19.

The eel terrine?
Turn to 123.

A bowl of peas?
Turn to 159.

A briar beast?
Turn to 25.

Or you could decide not to poison anything?
Turn to 234.

80

You enter the throne room, a grand airy chamber with walls inset by darkly shining onyx murals, and tall windows looking out over the wood-studded landscape to the north. At the far end stands a looming black throne with a row of spikes across the top, upon which are impaled skulls in various states of decay. Mal sits beneath them, unbothered by the occasional falling droplet of congealed blood, while Nefarian has dragged a lesser chair to his feet, and other dignitaries cluster about listening to their conversation.

As you glide towards them, Mal notices you. 'Ah, Mr Artanon.'

Do you have PLENTY OF TIME?
Turn to 134.

If not, and MAL IS IRKED with you ...
Turn to 175.

If neither of these is the case ...
Turn to 201.

81

Strike the note that says the chosen zagga is BLACK AND YELLOW. The one which will now be used in the ceremony is RED AND GREEN.

Turn to 49.

82

You move towards the dungeon door, but Haiken does not budge from blocking it.

'I must ask you stop right there, sir,' he says. 'The dungeon is off limits at the moment.'

You arch an eyebrow - nowhere in the castle is off limits to you. After all, *everything* needs dusting from time to time.

If you are an INTIMIDATOR, you could try bullying your way past Haiken?
Turn to 115.

If a DIPLOMAT, you could try to reason with him?
Turn to 169.

Or you could shrug and go back to bed?
Turn to 72.

83

As the chanting grows louder, you glance around at the rapt faces of the crowd. You see Mr Feralis standing towards the back, a happy grin on his wolfish face as he rests his paws on a bulging stomach. His lolling tongue finds a morsel stuck on his hairy chin, and licks it up into his mouth.

It seems that Feralis has received your gift, and made a bloody meal of it. You are glad to see him calm and content in the face of this low and powerful moon.

You nod in satisfaction and turn back to watch the ceremony continue.

Turn to 42.

84

You open the adjoining door to Nefarian's quarters and see Jilly using giant forceps to place a bedbug in a sack that wriggles and squeaks.

'Quickly,' you say, 'help me with this room.'

Together you strip Rostolph's bed and hunt down the remaining bugs, which are hiding under sheets and in pillowcases, angry to be disturbed.

'You've done well,' you tell Jilly. 'I won't forget this. Now, we had best let Lord Nefarian and his servant back in.'

You go to the adjacent guest quarters to find Nefarian sitting on an unmade bed while Rostolph stares out a window.

'Sirs,' you say, 'again, my unapologetically vast apologies. Your rooms are now free of bugs, I guarantee it.'

'You had better be right, Mr Artanon,' says Rostolph, rubbing his bite mark.

'Our thanks,' says Nefarian.

The two of them re-enter their rooms and shut the doors.

So, that was all quite exciting, eh, Mr Artanon?

Quite enough for one day – time for you to get some rest.

Turn to 96.

85

'Mr Feralis, if I may speak confidentially,' you say, drawing him aside. 'We are old friends, are we not?'

'Aye, Mr Artanon.'

'Well, although such things are not usually

spoken of in polite company, everyone has their own special ... wants, do they not? Peculiar tendencies which occasionally must be seen to, lest they build up and affect one's concentration. I have myself noticed you eyeing off the castle cats on occasion, have I not?'

Feralis looks abashed.

'There is no shame, Mr Feralis. We do not choose the way we are made.'

'So what is your business with this girl?'

'Every so often I go to the dungeon and choose a prisoner no one will miss. I tell them I'm going to help them escape, then bring them to the wall and over we climb. Only on the other side do I reveal my true intention – to *hunt them,* Mr Feralis.'

'What?'

'We are more alike than you thought. The look in their eyes when they realise I am no ally, but a foe after all - imagine it, sir. I give them a head start, then pursue and take my pleasure. None ever escapes me, I can assure you.'

Feralis grins. 'I had no idea, Mr Artanon, you sick puppy.'

'And I would like to keep it that way. You know how it is – a man in my position can't be seen attending to his baser desires. It is only every now and again, when the urges become too much to withstand. Can I trust you with this secret, Mr Feralis?'

'Of course, sir. Mum is the word.'

You rejoin Roseblossom. 'Come – I have spoken to my friend, and he will tell no one of our passing.

Turn to 193.

86

'It is my great pleasure to serve Lord Malacandros,' you state matter-of-factly. 'And if, on occasion, there's a little extra work involved, why, I didn't get where I am today by shirking.'

Rostolph goes quiet.

'I imagine you're much like me, Mr Rostolph. A butler's gaze must be far reaching, to make sure his staff all play their proper parts ... but that can give one a headache, which at times must be let out as steam. Am I correct?'

Rostolph chuckles. 'I believe you are.'

'So, it must be quite a relief to be away from Vorganis Castle for a few days. Leave the headache to another and let your time with us prove easy and refreshing.'

'Thank you, Mr Artanon.'

Rostolph seems thoughtful, but somehow more relaxed. At any rate, he's no longer trying to bait you into treasonous talk of Malacandros.

Turn to 52.

87

Hesitantly you unstop the bottle and pour a small glass of thick, viscous liquid. Well, Mr Artanon, it's now or never!

You tip back the drink and gag instantly. Whoever Mrs Plugberry is, she has a strange comprehension of what makes a person feel nice. This vile medicine is not for fine guests, that is certain!

Next, do you try:

The *Graveyard Pearl* Black Sauvignon?
Turn to 197.

The Sparkling *Bloodworm's Rest* Cabernet?
Turn to 111.

Nargletarg's Vineyard Dry Blue?
Turn to 224.

Glasscandle's Premium Scorpion Whisky?
Turn to 14.

Or pile up a cart full of booze and get out of here?
Turn to 168.

88

In the lead-up to the Stygias Ceremony, there is plenty of preparation to be done!

Do you want to check in with Bojanda, the castle tailor, to make sure the proper adjustments are being made to Mal's ceremonial robe?
Turn to 6.

Or visit Molsk in the aviary, where Lord Nefarian will arrive by wyrm tomorrow?
Turn to 133.

You could meet with the groundskeeper, Mr Feralis, and inspect the castle grounds, where the ceremony will take place?
Turn to 51.

Or speak with the head housekeeper, Mrs Bleakheart, who is in charge of preparing rooms for a multitude of important guests?
Turn to 272.

89

Mal doesn't even look at the tray – his attention is all on you.

'This is a disappointing performance, Mr Artanon, and not your first in recent times.'

'I swear, my lord,' you say, 'if I fail you again, I will cut my own liver out with a rusted blade and offer it to you before I die.'

Nefarian has been paying attention to the exchange, and, as Mal sits wondering whether to hurl you through the window or not, he clears his throat.

'Dear Cousin,' he says, 'I have a unabashed love of spike berries, and I don't think I'm alone. I'm actually amazed to see such excellent specimens so far out of season! You are a powerful lord indeed, unbeholden to the laws of time and nature.'

Mal is distracted by the onslaught of praise, and some of the fire goes out of his eyes.

'Serve them the damned berries,' he growls at you, and you waste no time obeying.

You shoot Nefarian a thankful look, and he gives you an almost imperceptible nod. Why he interceded to help you is uncertain, yet you are IN NEFARIAN'S DEBT.

Turn to 17.

90

You drift easily into slumber, and dream a happy dream about Brightlanders being murdered in their homes.

You are WELL RESTED.

Turn to 2.

91

Repugnis nods eagerly, which ripples his many chins. 'Yes sir, of course! Let me see now ...' He glances around and spots a bench where several platters are being assembled. 'Ah! How about some pickled rat heads and delectable carpaccio of slug?'

'Very good,' you say. 'I am told that Captain Haiken is particularly partial to rat. But see that you hurry along now, Repugnis. I don't need to remind you that his lordship's patience is virtually non-existent.'

'Of course, sir, of course.'

You click your fingers at some waiting footmen and they leap to action, seizing the platters and heading for the door.

It seems you are a DIPLOMAT.

Turn to 200.

92

So, having spent the afternoon however you chose, with frightening regularity it is dinner time again. Staff are moving upstairs towards the kitchens, and Repugnis is frantically trying to get everything sorted for the increasing-by-the-hour number of guests.

Do you have KNOWLEDGE OF FOUL PLAY?
Turn to 43.

Otherwise ...
Turn to 265.

93

'Ah, my good Miss Molsk,' you say, as you turn to lead her towards the wyrm pens, 'I cannot help but admire the fine steeds in your care.'

'I can see why, sir,' Molsk agrees enthusiastically. 'Wyrms are such graceful, noble creatures.'

The wyrms spit and snap at each other, their yellow eyes full of malice.

You let Molsk move slightly ahead, and surreptitiously reach for your dagger.

'Have you ever flown upon one, Mr Artanon?'

'I have indeed. There is an exhilarating sense of the balance one must maintain in order to avoid a plummet to one's death.'

'My wings prevent me from appreciating the risk, sir.'

'Then let me give you something else to appreciate.'

You drive the dagger into Molsk's neck. She gurgles in surprise and stands there stuck, until you let go and send her staggering. She collapses, her blood spraying out across the floor to mix with the dung. Shakily she looks up at you with piteous incomprehension, while all around you aviary workers have quietly stopped whatever they were doing. Molsk tries to speak but can only dribble, red bubbles running down her chin. A moment later life fades from her eyes.

MOLSK IS DEAD.

You reach down and draw your dagger from her flesh. 'Who is second in charge here?'

It is with some disappointment that *another* harpy steps forward, though this one is younger and seems appropriately nervous.

'Your name?' you ask, as you wipe the blade

clean on a handkerchief.

'Nia, sir.'

'Well, Nia, better get this aviary cleaned up before his lordship's guests begin arriving, or I'll be back to have a similar chat with you. Understood?'

Nia nods earnestly. 'Yessir, Mr Artanon.'

'Good.'

You leave the aviary satisfied that the message has 'sunk in'. In fact you can now assume that the AVIARY IS CLEAN.

Turn to 124.

94

You take Rostolph by the shoulder and smile in a friendly manner.

'Now, sir,' you say, 'I simply insist. I don't want to seem in deficit of hospitality.' You tighten your fingers on Rostolph's shoulder, strong from years of polishing silverware. 'It would just not be fitting not to cater specifically to a lord of Nefarian's standing.'

You dig your fingers in around Rostolph's shoulder blades. The other butler barely suppresses a yelp – he is shorter and slighter than you, and looks up with barely disguised worry.

'He ... that is to say, Lord Nefarian ...' he winces. '... does very much enjoy an eel terrine.'

You release Rostolph, who winces again as blood rushes back into his squeezed flesh.

'You will make certain, Mr Repugnis,' you say, 'that eel terrine is on the menu.'

'Of course, sir! It will be my pleasure.'

If you were BONDED WITH ROSTOLPH you must now strike that note.

Turn to 241.

95

You clear your throat and speak softly.

'That little one there is your rat-head-eating-fork, my lord.'

Despite your attempt to be subtle, Mal registers the exchange and chortles.

Haiken, embarrassed to be found ignorant, frowns. 'I know what fork to use, you stupid butler! Begone before I stab you in the eye with it.'

With your lords served, you move back from the table to remain in waiting.

Turn to 18.

96

You enter your bedchamber leery of restlessness, given the many concerns running through your head. Thus, when you lie down, you are pleasantly surprised (or would be, if you were awake) to find yourself fast asleep.

Rest well, Mr Artanon. A new day beckons!

Turn to 3.

97

'How would you like that, Mr Feralis?' you ask. 'You wouldn't be able to polish your own marbles, let alone wreak havoc on the general populace.'

Feralis finally focuses on you – the idea of a pet cone seems to terrify him.

'You wouldn't ... do that ... would you?'

'I would if it stops you from ruining the ceremony,' you say. 'Slink away into the night if you can't behave.'

Feralis gives a frightened nod, and turns to bound off into the trees.

Turn to 42.

98

Feralis looks quite miserable.

'It's just,' he says, 'well, the Stygias Ceremony takes place under a full moon, which is also when my animal side becomes most difficult to control. I will crave to bound and hunt, yet I want to be on hand for the ceremony. I will have to contain my instincts.'

'Indeed. We must all be on our best behaviour for the ceremony, Mr Feralis.'

Feralis nods determinedly. 'I thought that if I hunt every night in the lead-up, perhaps I can sate my appetites in advance, somewhat.'

'Commendable of you to try and bridle your bestial nature, Mr Feralis.'

'It is a blessing and curse, Mr Artanon.'

You both chuckle at this.

You are now privy to FERALIS'S WOES.

You decide to leave him to it, and head back to the castle to get some rest.

Turn to 261.

99

'My,' you say, trying to sound convincing as you consider Molsk's cracked, fungus-encrusted claws, 'your claws have so much ... potential ... Miss Molsk! Imagine how they would shine after many hours of scrubbing the aviary floor clean of all organic material.'

'What?' says Molsk.

Even you have to admit that your supposed compliment and ulterior motive have not married well. You will have to try something else.

Do you grab Molsk by the neck and push her head into a pile of dung, to illustrate the disgusting state of the place?
Turn to 107.

Or, if you have really lost patience, why don't you reach for the dagger you keep about your person at all times, and stab her with it?
Turn to 93.

Or you could give up and leave?
Turn to 124.

100

All fall to a hush as, from the direction of the bestiary, there comes the roar of the approaching zagga.

'First among the beasts of Stygias!' announces Mal. 'As the zagga consumes the virgin, so too, through it, will our God consume her!'

The creature's roar comes again, closer this time.

If the PATH IS SAFE ...
Turn to 10.

Otherwise ...
Turn to 189.

101

Once Mal has eaten his fill, he instructs Captain Haiken to accompany him to the throne room. The Captain looks longingly at the remains of the briar beast, but wipes his chin and dutifully follows Mal. After they have gone, servants busy themselves clearing the table and cleaning up.

If the CHAIR IS DIRTY ...
Turn to 156.

Otherwise ...
Turn to 36.

102

You stop and bow as Nefarian passes. He gives you a vague smile, and you breathe a sigh of relief as he passes.
    It's probably time to you went and checked in at your office.

Turn to 142.

103

The stable doors creak as a great black wyrm with fiery eyes swoops through them to land heavily on the aviary floor. Upon it sits Lord Nefarian, tall and handsome in the saddle, wearing a vest over a short-sleeved shirt that shows off his well-muscled arms. He slides gracefully from his steed and shoots Mal an easy smile.

'Don't part your lips too wide, cousin,' Mal mutters to himself. 'You'll reveal the face behind.'

A second, smaller wyrm lands more clumsily behind the first, many bags and cases swinging from its harness. Upon it sits a slight, bald man in silver-seamed livery who, you reason, must be Nefarian's butler.

'Cousin!' exclaims Nefarian, approaching Mal with open arms. When Mal makes no motion to join in any embrace, Nefarian deftly turns his extended arms seamlessly into a gracious bow. 'Or, as I should more rightly call you, my lord! Either way, it is good to see you.'

'And you, Nefarian,' Mal says through gritted teeth.

Nefarian rises and gives the air a little sniff.

If the AVIARY IS CLEAN ...
Turn to 48.

Otherwise ...
Turn to 195.

104

You unlock the dungeon door with your master key, and enter a stone corridor. After secreting your cart o' booze in a shadowy nook, you make your way past cells in which chains rattle and skulls grin. From somewhere nearby you hear the sound of screaming – you guess the torture chamber staff are putting in some time after-hours.

'Help me, please ...' mumbles a prostrate figure, reaching through cell bars to paw at your shoes. You kick his hand away before he smudges their shine.

You turn down another passage and there, in the last cell of the row, is the imprisoned virgin. She sits upon a dirty pallet wearing a torn white dress, nothing else in her cell save a cracked jug of water. She looks up at you, her pretty face framed by tangled locks of blonde hair. As she rises to her feet, you have to admire her comely figure.

It's a shame she has to be executed.

'Sir,' she whispers, 'is it time?'

'No, miss,' you say. 'The ceremony is tomorrow.'

She steps up to the bars and presses against them, squeezing her breasts between.

'Have you come to rescue me?'

'I'm afraid not, miss.'

'They only want me because I'm a virgin,' she says huskily. 'If someone were to change that, I would be eternally grateful. My name is Roseblossom, by the way.'

She is very lovely, no doubt about it.

Are you DRUNK?
Turn to 248.

If not ...
Turn to 191.

105

You wend your way towards the heart of the chamber, where the biggest pots belch over the brightest flames.

'More sheets in this one!' barks Bleakheart, as she looms out of the swirling mists. 'And get these others drying before the hearth!'

Her apron is patchy with moisture, and her thick brow drips condensation as she furrows it in your direction.

'Mr Artanon,' she says. 'You have an unenviable talent, sir, of interrupting me at my busiest.'

'Just wanted to make sure you have everything you need, Mrs Bleakheart. With so many guests arriving, I have trails of footmen marching about like ants to a kill.'

'Indeed,' she replies. 'Perhaps you can extrapolate from your own experiences then, that my workload is likely to be overwhelming?'

Are you a DIPLOMAT?
Turn to 166.

Or an INTIMIDATOR?
Turn to 236.

106

You decide to make a pass through the dining chamber on your way, just to show your face and make sure both Nefarian and Rostolph are there. You enter carrying a tray of lizard tartlets, and tong them out onto guests' plates. Rostolph stands behind Nefarian's chair, ready to meet his every need. As you serve Mal he doesn't even glance at you – you feel confident that, amongst the chatter and revelry, the absence of one butler will not be missed. You leave and head towards Rostolph's quarters. Nodding at a patrol of guards in the corridor, you hope they do not double back through the guest quarters while you are breaking in.

You arrive outside Rostolph's door, and pull your master key from your pocket on a chain – a butler to the Dark Lord must have access to any room in the castle! Upon entering the room, you note nothing immediately suspicious. There is a table, a bed, shelves, cupboards, and an adjoining door to Nefarian's quarters. Rostolph's case is on the floor.

Where will you search first?

Under the bed?
Turn to 206.

In Rostolph's case?
Turn to 164.

In the cupboard?
Turn to 132.

107

'Look at this!' you say, seizing Molsk by the neck and forcing her head towards the ground. She gives a squawk, and is unexpectedly strong, but due to your station she dares not put up much of a fight. You shove her face into a mound of warm wyrm turd as if punishing a naughty puppy.

'You see it?' you growl. 'You think it's nice to leave such mess lying around for everyone to admire? Or do you think it's time that someone took some responsibility around here?'

'I'm sorry, Mr Artanon!' Molsk splutters. 'Please, let me go! I'll get the place in order, I promise!'

As you push her away, one of her filthy claws nicks your wrist. You rub the scratch absently as you watch her bob off to organise her workers.

Unbeknownst to you, a virulent infection has entered your bloodstream. No matter what choices you make from here on in, it will inevitably cause you a surprising and agonising death.

Your days of service have come to an end.

108

You bow your head. 'No, lord. I was just making sure your quarters are adequate to your needs.'

'Very kind of you, Mr Artanon. Perhaps you will join us for some tea?'

Are you IN NEFARIAN'S DEBT and BONDED WITH ROSTOLPH?
Turn to 269.

Otherwise, make your excuses and leave. It is time you checked in at your office.
Turn to 142.

109

You are not sure that picking out the right zagga beast for the Stygias Ceremony is anything life has really prepared you for, but a good butler must be willing to meet any challenge. Thus you head out the castle's back door into the southern grounds, and up a path toward the bestiary. The bestiary is a circular building made of enormous logs, standing on one of

109 (cont'd)

Cayfax Mountain's larger plateaus. Its grounds are littered with sheds, pits and fields where beasts are trained or broken, and while the winds this high are kind at carrying off any animal related funk, you still catch the occasional ripe waft. You approach the entrance arch, guarded by statues of rearing dragons, and stop a handler who is being dragged along by an enthusiastic attack turtle on a leash. He tells you where to find Jhurgle, and you head in.

There is no wind inside. The bestiary is essentially an enormous stable, and the air is pungent with fur, farts, sweat and faeces. Chaff litters the floor along passages between pens, from which beasts snarl, hiss and spit. Some are contained by low wooden fences, while others stare out of formidable cells of thick metal bars with bite marks in them.

You find the beastmaster standing at a fence that spans two pens, a thoughtful expression on his face. In one pen are a pack of briar beasts – hairless boar-like creatures with armoured skin and backward curving tusks – and in the other are feathertailed foxes, which are small with multicoloured fur, and feathers growing from their tails.

'Mr Jhurgle,' you say.

'Oh, hello, Mr Artanon.' He strokes his bushy black beard, and creases his bushier black eyebrows. 'I was just standing here wondering if I'll ever work out how to domesticate a fox. They say it can't be done, but they also said I'd never teach a banshee to sing in tune. At any rate, what can I do for you?'

Are you privy to FERALIS'S WOES?
Turn to 220.

Otherwise ...
Turn to 253.

110

Roseblossom rushes to her cell door.

'I knew you'd come back! You weren't going to stand by and let those bastards murder an innocent girl.'

Not so innocent, you think to yourself, as you unlock the door.

Wondering how it has come to this, you lead Roseblossom back to the dungeon entrance and peek out.

The corridor is deserted.

'I know a way out,' you say, 'and there aren't many people around this late. There will be guards, however. Just stay close to me.'

'Sir, I will do whatever you say.'

You make for the castle's back door, erring towards stairwells and side passages when you can, avoiding the most common patrol routes. Almost with disbelief you reach the back door without incident ... but now there is the matter of the guards standing outside it.

'Stay in the shadows,' you tell Roseblossom.

You burst through the back door, surprising two guards.

'Brightlanders at the front gate!' you exclaim. 'Who knows how they got this far undetected, but they are definitely attacking!'

This works well. The guards glance at each other and tear off down the corridor. It won't be long before they realise they've been duped.

You call Roseblossom from hiding and bundle her out into the night.

The best idea, you think, it to make for part of the castle wall which you know is overgrown with vines. You lead Roseblossom through the grounds towards it, and enter a copse of trees. With the wall in sight, you are dismayed to hear a snuffling coming from some brush. Mr Feralis, the werewolf groundskeeper, pokes his head out.

'Mr Artanon!' he says. 'What are you doing out here at this time of night? And who is ...'

His nose twitches as he stares at the girl.

'She smells of Brightlander,' he growls.

Are you a DIPLOMAT?
Turn to 85.

If not, do you tell Mr Feralis you are looking for a secluded place to have some cheeky outdoor fun?
Turn to 39.

Or try to kill him with your dagger?
Turn to 252.

111

You uncork a bottle of *Bloodworm* and, after letting it breathe for a bit, pour yourself a sample and sip it slowly. The taste is fruity, with hints of corpsewood, as well as bits of floating bloodworm. It's all a bit much, really – whoever the winemaker was, they got too carried away with their flavours.

Not one for the guests, you think.

Next, will you try:

The *Graveyard Pearl* Black Sauvignon?
Turn to 197.

Nargletarg's Vineyard Dry Blue?
Turn to 224.

Glasscandle's Premium Scorpion Whisky?
Turn to 14.

Mrs Plugberry's Make-Me-Feel-Nice Cure-All Tonic and Tile Cleaner?
Turn to 87.

Or pile up a cart full of booze and get out of here?
Turn to 168.

112

You move past the studiously uninterested Bleakheart to the pot from whence the squeaking comes, which a chambermaid called Jilly stirs with a wooden pole. From out of the stew of sheets a dark shape launches, splashes Jilly with boiling water, and lands on the floor. It is something like a large tic with jagged mandibles - steam hisses from the joints of its exoskeleton as it squeaks in pain and scrabbles at the ground with barbed legs.

'Bedbug,' explains Jilly.

Another bug launches and lands by the first, and the chambermaid sighs. She fetches a dustpan and broom, sweeps the bugs up, and empties them into a bin from which you can hear more scraping and clicking. Jilly rams the broom end down into the bin, pounding and crunching until all sounds cease.

It seems you have gained some gruesome KNOWLEDGE OF BEDBUGS.

You decide you don't want to be in this stifling room any more, and leave.

Turn to 124.

113

As is only fitting, you serve your master first. As you place the largest and juiciest rat heads before him, your first footman Kalag – a young fellow who shows much promise – moves to Haiken and starts laying slug meat on his plate.

'Er,' says Haiken, 'not too much slug for me, thank you – I have an allergy.'

Mal, who is in mid-chew, scoffs, and shoots a shard of half-chewed rat skull out of his nostril to ping off a wine glass.

'Rut me, Haiken,' he says. 'I've seen you rip the throat from a charging horse, yet you can't stomach a little slug?'

Haiken seems embarrassed. 'They give me hives, my lord.'

'Ha! Well, better get over there with some of his precious rat heads, Mr Artanon.'

You do as you are bid, and place the remaining rat heads on Haiken's plate. They are a little on the smaller side, and you notice a wistful look in Haiken's eye as Mal lifts another plump one to his mouth.

With your lords served, you move back from the table to remain in waiting.

Turn to 18.

114

You decide to speak to the goblin messenger whose life you saved.

'Sarka,' you bellow, 'fetch me Peedy!'

A short while later, Peedy appears at your door

clutching his feathered hat to his chest.

'Mr Artanon, sir,' he says, 'I don't know how to thank you for interceding on my behalf with his lordship.'

You lean back in your chair and steeple your fingers.

'I do.'

'Pray, how can I be of service?'

'Tell me everything you learned about Lord Nefarian during your visit to Vorganis Castle.'

'Well, sir, as I'm sure you realise, a professional messenger does not dally long at any destination!'

'Indeed. However ...'

'However,' Peedy steps closer and lowers his voice, 'I can tell you that Nefarian has a confidante whom he trusts above all others – who spends most waking hours with him, and has an ear to all his plans.'

'Yes?'

'His name is Rostolph, and he's Nefarian's evil butler.'

You frown. 'This is not terribly enlightening. All dark lords have an evil butler. I am one myself, after all.'

'Ah,' says Peedy, 'but sir, Rostolph is an *evil*, evil butler.'

You ponder this a moment. It could be that you formulate some SUSPICIONS.

Out in the common room there sounds an unmistakable chime in the bell array – a summons to Mal's bedchamber. Wondering where the day has gone, you dismiss Peedy and exit your office.

Turn to 58.

115

'Now look here, Captain,' you say. 'Out on the battlefield you might be the belle of the ball, but inside this castle you have no say over my comings and goings.'

Haiken gets a thuggish expression on his face, which was already quite thuggish to begin with.

'If I was a servant who valued my mortal soul,' he says, 'I would not speak to a superior officer, *not to mention* a noble, in such a fashion.'

You sneer. 'If you think a trumped-up sword swinger who fell from his mother in some backwater ruin has any right to threaten the butler to Lord Malacandros himself, you really are as stupid as you look.'

The Captain gets a dangerous look in his eyes. 'What did you say about my mum?'

He draws his sword, and you wonder if you have made a mistake.

'That wasn't really the point,' you squeak.

As he runs cold steel through your chest, all doubt about mistake-making is certainly cleared up.

Your service ends here.

116

What will you say to calm Feralis down?

'Try to think harmonious thoughts, sir. It won't kill you to miss one night roaming the woods.'
Turn to 215.

'I think I can smell something in the trees, Mr Feralis. A fat briar beast, perhaps?'
Turn to 264.

117

Your well rested ears pick up the sound of someone approaching - it's a good thing you got such a good night's sleep! You slip through an adjacent door into what you know to be an unoccupied guest room and peer through its keyhole, which is apparently habit forming behaviour. You watch the outside corridor where you were but moments before.

Lord Nefarian arrives outside Rostolph's door and knocks.

'Mr Rostolph! Are you there?'

Rostolph opens the door and ushers his lord quickly inside, which strikes you as oddly familiar conduct, likely to get you killed should you ever treat Mal the same way.

Do you risk returning to Rostolph's keyhole and continuing your surveillance?
Turn to 196.

If you decide you've taken this far enough, go and check in at your office.
Turn to 142.

118

'Molsk!' you call. 'Where are you?'

A fluttering sounds from somewhere far above, where more cages hang from the roof, and Molsk descends to land before you. She is a harpy – half bird and half humanoid – with chipped claws, mottled brown-grey feathers, her skin speckled with downy fluff (the harpy equivalent of dandruff), and breasts that are distinctly hairy around the nipples.

Her only saving grace, as far as you can tell, is her affinity with creatures of the air.

'Mr Artanon,' she croaks, head bobbing like a vulture. 'To what do I owe the pleasure?'

'You are aware,' you say, 'that many distinguished guests will be arriving over the next few days for the Stygias Ceremony? Including his Wrathfulness's own cousin, Lord Nefarian?'

'Yes,' she replies. 'What of it?'

'Perhaps you could try to comprehend, somewhere deep within that thick skull of yours, that not everyone enjoys being assaulted by the funk of a thousand avian bumholes?'

Molsk blinks at you blankly.

You don't think reason is going to work, and decide to try a different tact.

Do you order Molsk to get the aviary in order, or else?
Turn to 12.

Do you grab her by the neck and push her face into a pile of dung, to illustrate the disgusting state of the place? This will mean touching her, which you are not entirely comfortable with.
Turn to 107.

Or do you try and flatter the moronic birdbrain?
Turn to 228.

119

'Ah,' you say. 'You have already told me of your woes, Mr Feralis. The coming moon still troubles you?'

'Aye, Mr Artanon. I've been thinking that if I hunt every night in the lead-up to the ceremony, I may be able to sate my instincts in advance, somewhat.'

You nod. 'Commendable of you to try and bridle your bestial nature.'

'It is a blessing and a curse,' he says.

You both chuckle at this.

You decide to leave him to it, and head to bed.

Turn to 261.

120

A smile spreads across Mal's face. 'Do you really think so?'

'Certainly, my lord – your rear is fearsome in the extreme, and will strike fear into all who behold it.'

Mal nods in satisfaction. 'You always know the right thing to say to make a dark lord feel good, Mr Artanon. And feeling good is looking good.'

If MAL IS IRKED, you may strike this note, as all is now forgotten.

Turn to 160.

121

'I believe a fox sounds like the ticket,' you say. 'You're sure they're very hard to catch?'

'Oh, indeed,' says Jhurgle. 'Mr Feralis will work up quite a sweat chasing one of those around.'

'Excellent. Please have one sent to him with instructions to release it tomorrow at dusk. That should give him ample time to gnash his teeth before the ceremony.'

You have SECURED A FOX for Feralis.

'Now,' says Jhurgle, 'what else did you want to speak to me about?'

Turn to 253.

122

You give the door a polite rap. Inside you hear a faint scuffling, and a sound like something wooden closing. Rostolph opens the door rather red-cheeked and dishevelled, but he smooths his livery when he sees you.

'Mr Artanon,' he says. 'I didn't think I would shee ... *see* ... you again so soon! To what do I owe the pleasure?'

You had better think of something to say, hadn't you?

'I wish to make certain all is satisfactory with your quarters, sir.'
Turn to 185.

'I want to ask you where you sourced such beautifully dark material for your livery – it makes mine look like a very ordinary midnight void.'
Turn to 247.

'What, in the name of Stygias, do you think you are doing smuggling live balfrog tadpoles into your room? Answer me, sir! Is it some weird sex thing?'
Turn to 263.

123

Repugnis calls for help getting another briar beast out of the oven, and all staff abandon the bench. Quickly you whisk out the jar and pour red powder over the eel terrine. For a moment it sits brightly upon the shimmering surface, and you worry that Repugnis will sense tampering with his dish ... but then it dissolves into the glistening oil and you breath a sigh of relief.
　　The EEL IS DUBIOUS.

Turn to 262.

124

How are you faring for time, Mr Artanon? Should you be going to check in at your office yet?

Do you have TIME FOR TWO THINGS?
Turn to 205.

Or TIME FOR ONE THING?
Turn to 231.

125

With some trepidation you bow deeply before Malacandros.
　　'If you are not capable of doing your job,' Mal says quietly, 'what is the purpose of keeping you in my employ?'
　　'My humblest apologies, oh Unforgiving One. I foolishly entrusted the cleaning of your chair to

another, and ...'

'Yes, that was not the first time you have been foolish today.'

'Please, lord, I ...'

Mal waves dismissively, cutting you off. For a blessed moment you think that he is finished with you. Then an amazing sort of pain blossoms in your stomach, and you look down to see flames bursting out from under your clothes.

'Master,' you cry, but it is too late.

It seems you have embarrassed Mal sufficiently to earn yourself a painful death.

Your service is at an end.

126

You enter the common area to find everyone industriously shining up candelabra and teapots. When they see you, all rise.

'Can anyone explain to me,' you say, 'why Sarka is sullying our cleanly swept corridor with a trail of sadness?'

Servants shift their feet uncomfortably and avoid your gaze.

'Mr Kalag?'

'Er ...'

'Er?' you repeat. 'Have I not taught you to speak clearly when addressed, sir?'

'Pardon me, Mr Artanon. What I meant to say was, Sarka was just a bit upset with the discussion we were having.'

'Which was?'

'Well, sir ... no one in particular was just remarking upon the fact that Mr Rostolph, sir, not to spread malicious gossip, sir, but that he must be very loyal to Lord Nefarian indeed – what with his lordship having recently executed Mr Rostolph's own brother. For every good reason, I have no doubt,' he adds quickly.

If you did not already, you now know about ROSTOLPH'S BROTHER.

'I see. I am confused, however, about what this has to do with Sarka.'

'It's just, Mr Artanon,' pipes up a kitchen maid, 'that she recently lost her own brother to heartworm, so the subject stirred up painful memories.'

'Fascinating,' you say. 'Well, I am sure no one is letting this dangerously idle talk interfere with their duties?'

There is a chorus of 'no, sirs', and you nod.

'Right then. Get back to it.'

Turn to 211.

127

'Kalag!' you snap, and your first footman miraculously materalises. 'Show Mr Rostolph to Lord Nefarian's guest chamber.'

Kalag nods dutifully and – much to your chagrin – offers to help Rostolph with the bags.

'We will speak later then, Mr Artanon?' asks Rostolph.

'Doubtlessly.'

You make your way towards the kitchens with PLENTY OF TIME.

Turn to 181.

128

Well, you've been a bit CLUELESS, haven't you, Mr Artanon?

Turn to 221.

129

You decide to clear your head with some fresh air and a constitutional. You enter the castle grounds and step off the path between hedges cut to look like horrible claws grasping at the sky. Ahead of you, at the edge of a cliff, you notice the distinctive silhouette of Mrs Bleakheart smoking an enormous, blazing pipe. Perhaps you should join her and take in the lights of Cayfax Town?

As you walk towards her, however, you pass some bushes in which you hear a rustle, and a low growl.

Do you investigate the bushes?
Turn to 67.

Or leave well enough alone, and continue on to broad-shouldered Mrs Bleakheart?
Turn to 172.

130

Strike the note that says the chosen zagga is RED AND GREEN. The one which will now be used in the ceremony is BLACK AND YELLOW.

Turn to 49.

131

'Ah,' says Haiken, relaxing his stance, 'It's Mr Artanon, is it not? I feel I must thank you for your ... subtlety ... at lunch today.'

'Think nothing of it, Captain. Just doing my job.'

'I was raised a lord, you know, but I'm afraid life as a soldier has erased some of my tableware lessons.'

'I understand, sir. Someone has to keep those filthy Brightlanders drowning in pools of their own blood.'

'Indeed.' He gives you a friendly nod. 'And what brings you out at such an hour in your bedclothes?'

'I am embarrassed to admit it, but I ate a lot of cheese shortly before bed. It was a poor choice, evidently made by someone completely bereft of his common sense.'

'Ha! Well, don't be too hard on yourself. I once shoved a sword through my best friend's back when I mistook him for my brother. We all make mistakes.'

'Indeed. But I was thinking of taking in the calming air of the dungeon.'

Haiken's brow furrows. 'I would ward you off that, Mr Artanon, if I could.'

'Oh?'

'The virgin for the Stygias Ceremony is imprisoned within. She is quite lovely, for a human that is, ahem, and has been attempting to use her wiles to save herself. For if, come the ceremony, she is no longer a virgin ... well ...'

'I take your meaning, Captain.'

'Best not to place yourself in way of temptation, eh?'

'Most wise, I am sure.'

Consider yourself WARNED BY HAIKEN.

'Well,' you say, 'perhaps this chat is all I needed. I should probably try and get some sleep.'

'Good night, Mr Artanon.'

You traipse back to your bed and eventually fall into a fitful slumber, in which you dream of trekking through a bizarre yellow landscape studded with triangular mountains full of holes.

Turn to 2.

132

You open the cupboard and there, nestled amongst hanging shirts, is the box you recognise from your keyhole espionage.

Well, you're never one to argue when things are too easy.

Carefully you open it, and there inside, along with other vials and jars, is the poison.

Put whatever you chose into the box and take the poison.

You now POSSESS POISON.

With your mission complete, it's probably time you got out of here!

Are you a BEDTIME RAIDER?
Turn to 84.

Otherwise ...
Turn to 208.

133

You head through the upper levels of the castle towards the aviary, and enter a corridor with a tattered look to it – tapestries with frayed edges, carpet that's been pecked at, the occasional white streak down the wall – all evidence of regular escapees.

Stepping through an archway, you enter a large and airy chamber that is aviary itself. Cages stacked everywhere contain all manner of squawking and shrieking winged creatures. Opposite you are pens where the wyrms are stabled – serpentine beasts with dragon-like wings which travellers ride all over Nocturnia. Along the outside wall are differently sized wooden shutters for differently sized aviary denizens, as well as a larger set of double doors that open onto a dark and stormy sky. Despite the breeze that blows through them, there's a stench in the air not easily ignored – a combination of dung, damp, rotting fruit and mould. Even as you watch, a wyrm being led to a pen defecates in the middle of the floor, and no one rushes to immediately mop up.

What do you do?

Go the stable doors and take a look over the land?
Turn to 69.

Inspect some of the caged creatures?
Turn to 5.

Shout for Molsk, the head of the aviary, to attend you?
Turn to 118.

134

You pour flutes of sparkling black and offer them to Mal's guests.

'Mmm,' says Nefarian, swirling his glass. 'An excellent vintage, lordship.'

'Of course,' says Mal. 'Nothing but the finest.'

You approach the throne to give Mal his glass and offer him the platter.

Are you serving a CHEESE SUBSTITUTE?
Turn to 270.

Otherwise ...
Turn to 17.

135

'They call me Schazelburkus,' you say, as you run your fingers up her hip and bunch her dress.

You have made up A SILLY ALIAS.

Turn to 258.

136

You follow a pathway out of the clearing towards the bestiary, which is paved by wide flat rocks.

'Cut extra large,' points out Feralis, 'so the bigger brutes do not dislodge them.'

'I understand that a zagga beast will be required for the ceremony?'

'Indeed, sir. Favoured by Stygias, those critters, though they're not as vicious as many think. Unless they're hungry, of course - but like many big predators, they only need to eat, oh, once a week or so. If they're well fed, they won't chomp on anyone else.'

You feel a rock sink under your foot, while the other end rises out of the ground.

'Loose,' you observe, and Feralis looks abashed.

'Thank badness you were here, Mr Artanon, or I'd have had no idea. Those zaggas aren't exactly light on their feet - I'd not like to risk one stepping on that.'

'Then don't, Mr Feralis.'

'I'd like to get some of my workers here right away while the light is good, sir, to check that every pebble and stone is secure.'

'I shall leave you to it, then.'

You head back to the castle, glad to know that the PATH IS SAFE.

Turn to 124.

137

While everyone bustles about readying for dinner, you instruct Kalag to send for Peedy. When the messenger arrives, you steer him into a less hectic corner.

'I have a job for you,' you say. 'It will nullify your debt with me.'

'Mr Artanon?'

'Here is my master key – be sure not to lose it. Use it to get into Mr Rostolph's quarters.'

Peedy goes a bit pale, and you take him by the shoulder.

'The very sanctity of the castle is at stake, Peedy.

It's of the utmost importance that you do what I ask. In days to come, Malacandros himself will reward you. Doesn't that sound good?'

Peedy nods uncertainly.

'Very well - here's what you must do. Somewhere in Rostolph's quarters is a box containing a jar of red dust. You must exchange it with this (you press whatever you have chosen to leave in the poison's place into his hand), and leave no other trace behind. In and out, Peedy, then bring me the dust in my quarters. Do you understand?'

'Yes, Mr Artanon.'

'The onyx will spill through your fingers if you get this right, Peedy. Now, go swiftly, while all are at dinner.'

Peedy gets a determined look on his face, and off he goes.

You are a DELEGATOR.

Turn to 265.

138

'My dear sir, it is only fitting,' you say. 'You and your master are our esteemed guests. In fact, I should also ask if there's anything *you* would particularly like to eat, since we servants will be allowed to sample everything that's prepared – after our masters are seen to, of course. And Repugnis is an excellent cook.'

Repugnis beams at this rare praise, and Rostolph licks his lips.

'I myself,' you say, 'would like to put in a request for parboiled crow eggs.'

'That does sound nice,' says Rostolph. 'As for me,

I have noted that spinach and goat spleen soup is on the menu. I certainly would not mind if some of that was left over!'

'I will ensure a bowl is reserved just for you,' says Repugnis proudly, and Rostolph nods with anticipation.

If you are not already, you can consider yourself BONDED WITH ROSTOLPH.

You somehow forget, caught up in the flow, that you have not in fact discovered what Nefarian's favourite dish is.

Turn to 241.

139

'Ho there,' you say, approaching the guard, who peers at you with piggy eyes from under his helm.

'Mr Butler,' he grunts.

'Have you not heard that a zagga has broken out of the bestiary? All guards are being called on to help recapture it.'

The orc looks uncertain. 'I have strict orders from Captain Haiken not to leave my post. Only he can relieve me.'

'Haiken is headed to the bestiary himself. Don't you understand, you brainless lug? The escaped beast is a part of the ceremony tomorrow! Then again, I suppose I could explain to Lord Malacandros why you failed to act in such an emergency. I can't imagine how he will reward your diligence – have you boiled in their own blood, perhaps? No, that seems too generous.'

The orc goes a paler shade of green. 'The bestiary, you say?'

'You are quick to cotton on, sir.'

The guard jogs off hurriedly, and you sigh with relief. You enter the dungeon, and head towards Roseblossom's cell.

Turn to 110.

140

You grab Repugnis by the front of his apron.

'Now listen to me, you quivering mound of gelatinous blubber carved to look like a person.'

Repugnis seems quite hurt. 'I can't do nuthin' about my weight,' he says.

You shake him, snapping his eyes to yours.

'Tomorrow night,' you say, 'is the most important feast of your miserable existence ... and yet your larder is missing something as fundamental as cheese?'

'I'm ... I'm sorry, Mr Artanon.'

'You see to it that some form of cheese finds its way into this kitchen by dinnertime or, Stygias help me, some kind of knife is going to find its way into you. Understood?'

'Yessir! I'll make it a priority.'

'You do that. Now, what else do you have to cover this gaping void in the nibblies department?'

After a quick scrabble around the benches, Repugnis puts together a tray of spikeberries and dried meat. You can only pray, as you leave the kitchen and head upstairs, that Mal will be satisfied with a CHEESE SUBSTITUTE.

Turn to 80.

141

What measures have you taken to help Mr Feralis?

If you have SECURED A FOX …
Turn to 34.

If you have SECURED A BRIAR BEAST …
Turn to 83.

If you used THE SARKA SOLUTION …
Turn to 286.

If you have done nothing yet …
Turn to 9.

142

In your office you find a stack of letters on the desk, none of which seem especially urgent. Still, you wouldn't mind going through them – unless you have a more pressing task?

Have you been ordered to CONSULT WITH JHURGLE?
Turn to 109.

Otherwise, rest your heels and open the letters.
Turn to 244.

143

Mal grins. 'Do you really think so?'

'Yes, Your Tastelessness. What greater insult than showing up to breakfast in last century's fashion? Especially when we can prophesy that your guests will be done up like peacocks in heat.'

'I like the tenor of your thinking, Mr Artanon.'

If MAL IS IRKED with you, you may strike the note.

You excuse yourself to go and oversee breakfast preparations.

Turn to 187.

144

Despite your misgivings, you give a globe a good hard shake and stare into its depths.

The snow swirls and forms into words, which sparkle and glow:

> *If you leave her just one thing, at least make it your name.*

No kind of real prophecy, just some vaguely general advice, no doubt designed to make the superstitious believe they have been told something deep and worthwhile.

You grimace, embarrassed to have even tried this silly toy, and push it away.

Discover the future in your own good time, Mr Artanon.

Turn to 92.

145

Stopping Mal once his mind is set on something is no easy task.

Are you a DIPLOMAT?
Turn to 186.

Do you want to try reason?
Turn to 30.

Or will you try to divert Mal's attention somehow?
Turn to 282.

146

Mal frowns at his posterior a bit, then nods.
    'As you say, Mr Artanon. I can work with this.'

Turn to 160.

147

The black and yellow zagga has a mean look in her eye as she lowers her snout to the sacrifice. She takes a deep sniff, savouring the scent of her meal-to-be. The sacrifice begins to wail, but is abruptly cut off as jaws clamp down over her torso. Her legs kick as blood sprays all over the altar, soaking into the stone, spilling down the sides in torrents.

It must be asked again – have you DEFLOWERED THE VIRGIN?
Turn to 53.

Of course not! How dare you.
Turn to 209.

148

'Would you like to see a selection, Mr Artanon?'

Your fondness for cheese overtakes you, and you sample slice after slice from a large platter. Repugnis watches curiously as you well and truly overdo it, filling your belly with a creamy stew until you feel fit to curdle. Finally you manage to pull yourself away, and gurgle off towards your bedchamber.

You have EATEN A LOT OF CHEESE.

Turn to 261.

149

Your livery is not designed for scaling walls, Mr Artanon, and your well polished shoes are a bit on the slidey side. Your coattails flap in the wind, dragging at you and whipping your legs. Your pants are tight and do not allow for easy bending at the knees. As you move your hand to find purchase, a cuff-link snags a vine and you miss your intended handhold. You are sent entirely off balance, and are too constricted by clothing to recover. You fall to the mountainside and dash your brains out on the rocks.

You make a fine looking corpse, Mr Artanon.

150

You attempt to summon a smile for sallow-cheeked Mrs Bleakheart.

'You know,' you say, 'I find that vinegar often helps with the removal of stains from his lordship's garments.'

Bleakheart pushes the tablecloth further into her mouth and gives a good hard suck. She then removes it to show you that the stain is completely gone.

'I think you'll find I am rather acid-tongued, Mr Artanon,' she says.

You decide you don't really want to be in this stifling chamber any more.

Turn to 124.

151

'I see you've been practising croquet?' you observe.

'Yes indeed, sir, myself and some of my gardeners. The inter-castle championship is coming up soon and I don't want to score second place again.'

'It is commendable that you strive for excellence, Mr Feralis.'

Feralis's yellow eyes glint with worry. 'Oh, it's not that, Mr Artanon, laudable as you make it sound.'

'What, then?'

'I just don't want to win a ...' Feralis gives a shiver. '... *silver* medal again.'

You cannot help but chuckle.

Now, would you like to inspect the front gate?
Turn to 267.

Or the ceremony site?
Turn to 240.

152

With some trepidation, you bow deeply before Malacandros.

'If you are not capable of doing your job,' Mal says quietly, 'then what is the purpose of keeping you around?'

'My humble apologies, oh Unforgiving One,' you stammer. 'I foolishly entrusted the cleaning of your chair to another, and ...'

'Yes, that was foolish. I will look like a grubby child in front of my guests.'

'Please, lord, if you will just give me another chance ...'

'Out of my sight,' Mal growls, waving you away.

MAL IS IRKED with you.

Thinking it best to obey, you retreat from the dining chamber to your office until dinner is finished and Mal is on the way to bed. Hopefully, when he rises, all will be forgotten. Hopefully.

So, now what?

Will you retire to your own bed and ensure a good night's rest for the coming day?
Turn to 261.

If you are feeling peckish, you could visit Repugnis in the kitchen?
Turn to 40.

Or take a night time stroll in the castle gardens?
Turn to 129.

153

You check your supply ledgers for any deficits you might have missed in the lead-up to the ceremony. Although you are generally fastidious, especially so with a momentous occasion on the horizon, it does not hurt, you have found, to be a little paranoid.

As you peruse the pantry stocks you realise, to your great surprise, that there is a severe lack of cheese in the castle! Quickly you grab a quill and write a note to the cheesemaker down in Cayfax Town, then head to the common room and pull Sarka to her feet by the scruff of her neck.

'Deliver this message immediately and have them send up everything in their inventory.'

'Yessir, arf arf.'

You have ENSURED ADEQUATE CHEESE SUPPLY.

A chime sounds in the bell array, unmistakable to your ear – a summons to Mal's bedroom. Wondering where the day has gone, you exit the common room to go and help Mal dress for the evening.

Turn to 58.

154

Having discovered Nefarian and Rostolph's childish game, you figure there is no reason to let it ruin everybody's ceremony. If they know they are under suspicion, they will have little choice but to abort their plan, leaving no one but you any the wiser, and things can go on as normal.

You take a notebook from your pocket and pen a note which you hope will keep everything peaceful.

You are a NEGOTIATOR.

Turn to 235.

155

Mal doesn't even look at the tray – his attention is all on you.

'This is fairly disappointing, Mr Artanon. I was looking forward to a wedge of slurried red.'

'The problem is being rectified even as we speak, Your Peckishness.'

Nefarian has been paying attention to exchange, and clears his throat.

'Dear Cousin,' he says, 'I have a great love of spikeberries, and I don't think I'm alone. I am actually amazed that you have such excellent specimens so far out of season! You are a powerful lord indeed, unbeholden to the laws of nature and time.'

Mal is distracted by the onslaught of praise, and seems to forget about your galling inadequacy.

'Well,' he says, smiling magnanimously, 'berries for all, then!'

You hasten to echo his words with your actions. As you serve the guests berries you shoot Nefarian a thankful look, and he gives you an almost imperceptible nod. Why he interceded on your behalf you are not sure, yet you are IN NEFARIAN'S DEBT.

Turn to 17.

156

You give a sigh as you remember that the armrest of Mal's chair is stained. It will be a damnable job scrubbing it clean, for nothing marks worse than dragon bone. You aren't sure if you trust anyone else to do it, either. Goblins are not the most reliable creatures, and the only other human present is Kalag. You have errands for him to run, however, and would prefer not to keep him from them.

What do you do?

Not take any chances, and see to the cleaning personally?
Turn to 65.

Tell one of the stupid goblin servants to do it?
Turn to 259.

Delegate the task to Kalag?
Turn to 212.

157

You give a wry chuckle.

Mal stalks forward with flames building at his fingertips. 'You think this is funny, Mr Artanon?'

'What better way to honour the Shadow God, lord?' you say. 'Does he not preach that we all shall tend to our baser natures? That we shall be wicked, and true to our own dark hearts? That we shall murder without pity, steal without remorse?'

Mal looks uncertain. 'What of it?'

'To punish me for being the very thing the Shadow God decrees, on this auspicious occasion, may not be the best way to show deference to his wisdom. Not to mention sully the ceremony with an unsuitable death. Stygias may take umbrage, Your Cautiousness.'

Mal slowly lowers his hand, and the weight across your shoulders dissipates. You can see you have put doubt into his mind.

'Well, Mr Artanon,' he says, 'you had better have a swift solution. I probably don't need to describe the extent of my wrath if you do not.'

Are you aware of BLEAKHEART'S PREFERENCES?
Turn to 232.

If not, do you call for a virgin to come forth from the crowd and offer themselves as sacrifice?
Turn to 13.

Or do you point to one of the noble's young children?
Turn to 59.

158

'Ah!' Nefarian says brightly. 'Mr Artanon! I was hoping to bump into you.'
    'Sir?'
    'Come, share a pot of tea in Rostolph's quarters – I'm heading there just now.'
    'That is very kind, my lord, but ...'
    'Please, I insist.'
    Unable to refuse a direct request from a lord, you are obliged to do as Nefarian wants, and follow him into Rostolph's quarters.

Turn to 269.

159

Repugnis calls for help getting another briar beast out of the oven, and his staff rally to him. In their absence you whisk out the jar and empty it into the

peas. For a moment the red powder sits brightly upon their green faces, and you worry that Repugnis will sense tampering with his dish ... but then the poison dissolves in the butter and you breath a sigh of relief.
The PEAS WON'T PLEASE.

Turn to 262.

160

'Come,' says Mal, 'let us go and welcome another snake into the long grass.'
Accompanied by several honour guards, you and Mal make your way up to the aviary. You find it thrumming with activity - workers run about with squawking birds, the wyrm pens brim with serpentine steeds, and a plot of freshly arrived nobles has already thickened. They approach Mal bowing and scraping, while guards set about clearing an area before large stable doors in the outside wall.
'Hmm,' Mal says, glancing about, 'where's Molsk?'

If MOLSK IS DEAD ...
Turn to 202.

Otherwise ...
Turn to 250.

161

Listening to Sarka, you can't help but feel you have heard similar worries expressed quite recently.

'Mr Feralis shares your plight,' you say. 'It must be quite difficult for ... people ... such as yourselves, to fit into the norms of society when yellow faces light up the sky with surprising regularity.'

Sarka looks at you with a touch of wonder. 'I did not think a normal would understand what it's like.'

'Well,' you say.

Have you already SECURED A FOX or SECURED A BRIAR BEAST?
Turn to 73.

If not ...
Turn to 260.

162

'Well,' you say, 'I suppose there's no harm in a small sample, if Repugnis has enough to spare?'

'Oh, yes, Mr Artanon,' says Repugnis, always eager to please. 'Just give me a moment.'

He returns with a saucer upon which several beached balfrog tadpoles writhe and squeak.

'Be careful not to swallow them whole,' he warns. 'A live one could wreak havoc on your digestive tract with its tiny horns.'

You join Rostolph in taking a tadpole and raising it to your mouth. Being wary not to let it slip through your fingers, you catch its head between your teeth and clamp down hard. Liquid guts spray out across your tongue, which is quite a treat, to be sure.

'Excellent, Repugnis,' you say.

You turn to Rostolph to see if he agrees, but he has an odd expression on his face and a bulge in his cheek.

'Is everything all right, Mr Rostolph?' you ask.

'Yesh,' he says, covering his mouth. 'Jusht ... ah ... got a horn schtuck in my gum.'

'Oh dear,' says Repugnis. 'The dangers of fine dining, I'm afraid. Would you like to spit into a bowl?'

'No, no ...' Rostolph's eyes are watering, and you think you see movement along the inside of his cheek. 'Apologiesh, I don't think thish food agreesh with me.'

Without another word he walks stiffly out of the kitchen.

What was that all about, Mr Artanon?

Would you like to follow Rostolph?
Turn to 61.

If not, you could go and check in at your office?
Turn to 142.

163

Jhurgle is white as a swamp wraith. Meanwhile the zagga coughs up a hairball the size of a tumbleweed.

'Take her!' Jhurgle orders the handlers. 'I'll have another beast fetched immediately, lord, and this one will be ravenous, or I'll eat my ...'

'Feet,' offers Mal. 'Starting with your toes.'

Thus encouraged, the beastmaster hastens on his way.

Mal turns to the sky, where the skull gazes back and forth in confused annoyance. 'Oh Wondrously Short-Tempered God!' he calls. 'Damn us with your angry stare for just a little longer, I beg you. We just need to ... get things sorted out a bit.' He spins on the dark priests. 'Chant, vermin! Chant!'

Hurriedly the priests start chanting again, but it does not stop the air growing tenser with every passing moment. After what seems like an interminable wait, Jhurgle and his handlers reappear leading a BLACK AND YELLOW ZAGGA.

'The beast!' Mal cries, close to hysterics. 'It is nearly here, oh God! And nearer still! Oh, it is drawing so close to the altar now! It will be with us at any moment!'

He carries on like this until the replacement beast is in position.

'Okay!' says Mal. 'Now, unleash the bloody thing!'

Turn to 147.

164

You consider Rostolph's case carefully. Knowing what evil butlers are like, especially those with things to hide, you suspect it might be trapped. Warily you open it pointed away from yourself, lest some dart or dagger spring out ... but nothing happens. Still cautious, you turn the case around and look inside. A layer of clothing on top covers whatever is beneath, but you see no obvious signs of security. You reach in gingerly to move some of the clothing aside, and that's when you notice a greenish cobweb in the corner of the case. Your spider-farming knowledge kicks in too late, as a tiny hasp spider leaps out of hiding and sinks its fangs into, appropriately enough, the webbing of your finger.

'Well,' you say, 'hello, little one.'

It is lucky that, as a child, you were immunised against all kinds of spider bites – a painful process that nonetheless ensured your survival on a spider farm - and now seemingly again.

You palm the spider and search the case, which reveals nothing more condemning than a pink loincloth.

Gently you place the angry little spider back amongst the clothes, and close the lid.

Where to look next?

Under the bed?
Turn to 206.

In the cupboard?
Turn to 132.

165

'Sarka was supposed to take care of this,' you growl.

'Oh,' says Repugnis, 'come to think of it, Sarka did deliver a crate this morning. Where it is? Ah!'

Repugnis leads you to a crate by the wall, and prises the lid off to reveal wheels and wedges of cheese stacked on top of each other.

'Hop to it!' you snap, irritated that Repugnis is not aware of his own inventory. 'Get a selection prepared for his lordship this instant, and how dare you accuse me of polishing off at least the equivalent amount.'

'I, er ... said nothing of any specific amount.'

'I said hop to it!'

Repugnis leaps to action as if your words are reins on his behind, and soon enough you are heading upstairs with wine and a cheese platter piled nice and high.

Turn to 80.

166

'Well, Mrs Bleakheart,' you say, 'perhaps I can be of service? If you could use some more able bodies around here, for example, I'm sure I could source them for you.'

Bleakheart blinks as she takes this in, processing the information slowly and compiling her atonal response.

'Er ... yes, that would be helpful, sir. Thank you.'

She seems momentarily stunned by her own words, and you realise she must be stressed indeed.

You leave the cloudy washroom, seize a passing servant, and order him to round up some dogsbodies for Mrs Bleakheart.

Turn to 211.

167

'I realise,' you purr, 'that your sensory faculties are most likely clogged with your own putrefied brain matter, Miss Molsk, but for those of us still possessing a modicum of olfactory capability, the atmosphere in here is less than welcoming.'

Molsk blinks at you, clearly confused.

'It reeks,' you clarify.

Molsk gives you a yellow smile. 'Yes – lovely, isn't it?'

'Do you think the Dark Lord wishes to greet his esteemed guests in such an obnoxious environment? Do you imagine that he shares your own particular fondness for the stench of decay, or can you summon the requisite objectivity to envision an alternative preference?'

Molsk cocks her head uncertainly.

'Let me be completely transparent, Molsk, if indeed transparency is possible while clouded by the stink clouds emanating from your feculent carcass. If you do not get this place cleaned up immediately, I shall return to give *you* a bath.'

The feathers of Molsk's crest stand up straight.

'You ... you wouldn't.'

'On the contrary – I'll have you dunked in soapy water and scrubbed until you smell of roses. I'll have you patted dry with fresh towels, manicured and daubed with perfume.'

'No! No, Mr Artanon! Please, have mercy!'

'It's every inch of this place, or it's you. One or the other will be clean. Decide.'

'I'll do anything you ask!'

You are satisfied that Molsk has gotten the message. In fact you can now assume that the AVIARY IS CLEAN.

Onwards, Mr Artanon.

Turn to 124.

168

You load a cart with bottles and clink out of the cellar.

How many samples of booze did you try?

One or two?
Turn to 35.

Three or more?
Turn to 233.

169

'Now really, Captain,' you say, 'I am used to having the run of the castle, under the auspices of Lord Malacandros I hasten to remind you. I must ask why you would bar me from the dungeon, so to speak.'

The Captain is not amused by your silly pun. 'There is an important prisoner within, and I don't want her disturbed. She will need all her strength if she is to ... die horribly ... in two night's time.'

You assume he is talking about the Brightlander virgin he recently captured.

'And,' he adds, 'I am certain His Evilness would agree with my caution in this particular instance.'

Wary of the hard look in his eye, you decide it best not to press the issue.

'Well,' you say, 'I suppose I should probably try to get some sleep anyway.'

You traipse back to your bedchamber and eventually fall into a fitful slumber, in which you dream of trekking through a bizarre yellow landscape studded with triangular mountains full of holes.

Turn to 2.

170

You pore over the day's mail.

There is a bill for new scuttlefang traps ordered by Mrs Bleakheart, which should have gone to the castle treasurer, so you put it aside for redirection. A very politely worded note from Captain Erkenslaw, the head of the castle guards, asks you to put the annual Guardsman's Ball in your calendar – which you do, although it is months away and hardly an immediate concern. There are also some job applications for various household positions, which you consider with some interest, as you detest being short-staffed. You are just pondering whether a gargoyle could possibly make a good kitchen scullion – they move so slowly, after all – when you hear a chime in the bell array that is unmistakable to your ear. Wondering where the day has gone, you rise and exit your office, to go and help Mal dress for the evening.

Turn to 58.

171

Nefarian smiles. 'You are wise, Mr Artanon. Stick with me, and I promise you rewards beyond your comprehension. Just a little insurance policy, before we continue ...'

A sinewy scarlet thread curls from his fingertip. It snakes into your chest, and you gasp as a warm knot ties itself around your heart.

'What ... have you done ... lord ...'

'A simple precaution, Mr Artanon. Your heart is now linked to mine. If mine stops beating, so will yours.'

Powerful magic indeed – Nefarian is as skilled a mage as his reputation says.

You are BOUND TO NEFARIAN.

'So, you can see,' says Nefarian, 'it is now *undoubtedly* in your best interests that we succeed. Perform the task I give you, and I will undo the spell and shower you with riches.'

What else can you really say at this point?

'Very good, my lord.'

171 (cont'd)

Rostolph flips open a wooden box and takes out a jar of red powder. 'We intend,' he says, 'to use this virulent poison on Malacandros at the ceremony feast. I've been trying to work out which dish would be best to secrete it in, hence my interest in the balfrog tadpoles.'

'No good,' says Nefarian. 'Balfrog tadpoles are far too popular. I'll have allies at the feast, and it will look odd if they all refuse to partake of the centrepiece dish. Do you have any better ideas, Mr Artanon?'

'Peas,' you say, your tongue suddenly dry and thick in your mouth. You would prefer not to have been placed in this position. 'Malacandros loves peas.'

'Does he?' Nefarian screws up his face in distaste. 'I knew he was evil, but not *that* evil. Yuck. At any rate, that is excellent to know.'

'And you, sir,' says Rostolph, 'will be in an excellent position to sneak poison into the peas just before they are served.'

'Then Malacandros dies,' says Nefarian, 'I become Dark Lord, and a glorious new night falls over Nocturnia.'

You force yourself to smile. 'It will be a great relief to be rid of Malacandros.'

'You take care of your part, Mr Artanon,' says Rostolph, 'and we'll take care of the rest.'

He hands you the jar – you now POSSESS POISON.

As you leave Rostolph's quarters, you can only hope that you somehow manage to come through all this unscathed.

Best, in the meantime, to keep up appearances, and check in at your office.

Turn to 142.

172

You take a place upwind of Mrs Bleakheart, and the great clouds she puffs from her rubbery, protuberant lips. Beneath you, at the base of the mountain, glow the distant fires and slow-burning street lamps of Cayfax Town.

'Good evening, Mrs Bleakheart.'

The orc housekeeper spares you a sidelong glance. 'Mr Artanon,' she acknowledges.

'Taking in the night?'

'Just looking for some peace and quiet.'

Ignoring her unfriendliness, you press on. 'How go the preparations for our many important guests?'

'As well as can be expected.'

'Very well indeed then, in your capably large hands.'

'Mmf.'

You decide that you are getting very little value out of this exchange, and thus make your excuses to no further response.

It's time you were getting to bed anyway.

Turn to 261.

173

'A briar beast should do the trick,' you say. 'Dangerous prey will get his blood fired.'

'I imagine so,' says Jhurgle. 'Briars take some killing, that's certain.'

'Excellent. Please have one sent to Mr Feralis with instructions to release it tomorrow at dusk. That should give him ample time before the ceremony to wet his snout.'

You have SECURED A BRIAR BEAST for Feralis.

'Now,' says Jhurgle, 'what else did you want to speak to me about?'

Turn to 253.

174

'Please, my lord,' you whisper, 'this really is ...'

You want to say it is all Jhurgle's fault, for not watching his charge properly, or even Feralis's, for failing to check that the path was safe. However, given Mal *did* charge you with overseeing everything, the responsibility, when it boils down to it, is yours.

This is just before your blood begins to boil.

'A way to help us bide the time!' Mal informs the crowd. 'And whet the Shadow God's endless appetite for death!'

You cannot help but scream as you collapse to the ground. For some reason, the heat of your own bubbling blood is worst in your ears, as the tiny but distinct mechanisms of your eardrums warm up to a glow. It seems that Erkenslaw was right – this pain is certainly enough to recognise your own imminent demise.

Your service ends here.

175

Mal's eyes narrow to slits. 'I thought I made my desire for cheese fairly clear and present – wouldn't you agree, Mr Artanon?'

You experience a sinking feeling. 'Yes, my lord.'

'And yet you have kept my guests and I waiting

while you've been off, I don't know - catching butterflies and braiding their antennae?'

You decide not to point out how difficult and weird that would be.

As Mal's guests guffaw dutifully, Nefarian clears his throat. 'Come, Cousin, I'm parched for wine. I don't see how turning this fellow to cinders will solve my problem.'

Mal glares at you, and you half-expect to burst into flames right then and there. You also wonder why Nefarian would intercede on your behalf.

'Very well,' growls Mal. 'Hurry up and serve.'

You shoot a thankful glance at Nefarian, who gives you an almost imperceptible nod.

You are IN NEFARIAN'S DEBT.

Turn to 134.

176

You arrive outside the servant's common room just in time to see Sarka bound out with tears streaking down her whiskers, and run off down the corridor. Do you want to:

Enter the common area and see what's going on?
Turn to 126.

Follow the werewolf and find out what's the matter with her?
Turn to 242.

Loiter outside the common area and eavesdrop on what's being said?
Turn to 273.

177

You drop into step beside Rostolph.

'If I *could* tell you similar tales,' you reply pleasantly, 'I would probably opt not to, for fear my wagging tongue would end up sliced down the middle - thus ensuring the most offensive thing to spill from it thenceforth would be drool. I certainly wouldn't risk speaking out in front of a complete stranger, unless I wanted him to think me a simpleton, and prove himself one by believing me.'

Rostolph stares into the middle distance for a moment, then gives a sickly laugh.

'I shall have to watch myself around you, Mr Artanon.'

'I should imagine so.'

Turn to 52.

178

'I must apologise and take full responsibility, my lord,' you say. 'I will make certain that everything is brought up to scratch.'

'You do that, Mr Artanon,' Mal says. 'Otherwise I'll give you over to the whipmaster, and he does not believe in scratches, I can assure you.'

You nod, and gulp. 'Yes, my lord.'

Note that MAL IS IRKED with you.

Turn to 66.

179

Really, Mr Artanon? As the words begin to form on your lips, you realise that speaking them aloud will be akin to signing your own death sentence. Come now, sir, you can do better than this! At least play along with Nefarian for now, even if you intend to give him up later. Otherwise you may as well just stop reading now and assume that you die.

Turn to 171.

180

Malacandros raises his hands to the moon as the dark priests chant.

> *Deliver us from sun and light*
> *Deliver us eternal night*
> *When from life we disembark*
> *Take our souls into the dark*
>
> *Keep our hearts shrivelled and small*
> *Safe from goodness, one and all*
> *Safe from what is wise or right*
> *Lost in your eternal night*

That kind of thing.

Above the altar, dark clouds swirl before the moon without the aid of any wind.

There is no doubt that Stygias himself is present, and all around the excitement grows palpable. The unnaturally churning clouds in the sky coalesce with purpose, taking on the shape of a giant skull. Through its eye holes the moon glows brighter – the chilling gaze of Stygias himself. Never in all your nights have you ever been so awed.

'All hail Stygias,' you murmur.

'All hail, Stygias,' others say. 'All hail Stygias.'

Are you privy to FERALIS'S WOES?
Turn to 141.

If not ...
Turn to 9.

181

The kitchen staff are already busy with lunch preparations, and you slip between them to the wine cupboard. It's a bit early in the day, you think to yourself, but then again, a cheeky glass of vino at mid-morning does not land very high on the Dark Lord's list of crimes.

You collect a bottle of sparkling black from the cupboard (which, you note, is almost empty – time to bring more stock up from the cellar?) then grab Repugnis by the ear.

'I need a cheese platter for His Ravenousness.'

Repugnis looks about uncertainly. 'Hmm. I think we're running low on cheese, actually.'

Have you recently EATEN A LOT OF CHEESE?
Turn to 238.

Otherwise ...
Turn to 279.

182

You remember Captain Haiken's words, and decide it best not to tempt fate by entering the dungeon. Deliver your wine to the kitchen, then go to bed, Mr Artanon!

Turn to 96.

183

'Forgive me, oh Deprived One,' you say. 'I was merely ...'

'Save your excuses,' says Mal, his voice rising. 'It doesn't matter. You should have been here and you weren't. You have failed me in your duties for the last time, Mr Artanon.'

'But lord ...'

There is no reasoning with Mal at this juncture. With a dismissive wave, he turns your body inside out where it stands. The only saving grace is that your eyes pop in the process, so you can't see your own slowly beating heart quivering on display outside your busted rib cage.

Your service ends here.

184

You find the kitchen abuzz with activity. Benches overflow with food, workers bustle hither and thither, and Repugnis waddles about shouting orders and waving a spoon in the air.

'Guests are situated, Mr Repugnis,' you tell him. 'Are you ready to send starters?'

184 (cont'd)

'Yes, Mr Artanon, sir.'

Rostolph is still dithering, so you decide to put him to use.

'Here,' you say, handing him a tray of skewered newts, 'get these upstairs while they're hot.'

Rostolph nods and does as he's told.

You follow him up with your own tray, and find celebrations in full swing. You've put Kalag in charge of wine, so he patrols with a small army of servers on watch for empty glasses. The table is spread with the castle's finest crockery, and a hundred candelabra twinkle along its length. In a corner musicians play on spiky instruments, and scantily clad dancers twirl. Laughter echoes through the hall, and eyes light up at the sight of food arriving.

Mal sits at the head of the table, and beside him Rostolph whispers in Nefarian's ear. Nefarian nods, picks up a glass and taps it with a spoon.

'My lords and ladies! I would like to propose a toast ...'

As Nefarian speaks you notice Rostolph slink out, and something makes you decide to keep an eye on him. You head after him, back down to the kitchen, and catch up as he is speaking to Repugnis.

'... speechmaking in progress. Once that's done with, we shall want the mains to arrive promptly, yes? People will already be seated, so the timing will be good.'

To his credit, Repugnis glances to you for confirmation. You nod – Rostolph is an upstart for ordering around your staff, but you wonder if there is some reason for his timing.

Repugnis starts to ready the mains, including a huge tureen full of squirming balfrog tadpoles, an oily looking eel terrine, and several roast briar beasts.

Do you POSSESS POISON?
Turn to 79.

If not ...
Turn to 262.

185

'Very satisfactory indeed, for the both of us,' says Rostolph. He opens the door and ushers you into his room. It is adjoined to Nefarian's grander quarters by an ornate door that is currently closed.

'The bed is wide, the cupboards roomy, the fruit bowl fruited, the carpet fluffed. Your hospitality is faultless, Mr Artanon.'

You cannot see anything immediately suspicious about anything.

'I'm glad to hear it,' you say. 'Make sure to let the staff know if you're in any kind of want.'

'Will do, Mr Artanon, shall do. Now, unless there is anything else?'

You can't think of further reason to dally, but you make up your mind to watch Rostolph even more carefully. He is up to something, you just know it.

As you go to leave the room, you almost bump into Lord Nefarian.

'I hope I'm not interrupting anything?' he says calmly, entering.

Turn to 108.

186

You give a little cough, and Mal fixes upon you.

'Something to say, Mr Artanon?'

You give a small bow. 'Forgive my interruption, oh Murderous One. I merely wish to suggest that, if should I be allowed to discuss with this wretch of a messenger what he has observed of Lord Nefarian's habits during his visit to Vorganis Castle – after I have attended to your repast, of course – then I would be able to make certain that your beloved cousin's stay with us matches the standards to which he is accustomed. I would not, of course, use such information to ensure that Lord Nefarian is less than comfortable, by deliberately, for example, setting up his quarters in a fashion he would find undesirable, in a bid to shorten his stay with us here at Cayfax Castle.'

Mal frowns as he decodes what you have said, and then gives you a sly smile.

'Why, Mr Artanon. A most excellent suggestion.'

You bow again and turn to Peedy, who is clearly confused over why he's being spared.

'I will send for you once my lords are fed,' you tell him briskly. 'Now cease your bothersome loitering and begone.'

Peedy needs no further encouragement, and retreats hurriedly from the hall.

It seems that PEEDY LIVES.

Turn to 222.

187

Breakfast is rather a low key affair. Repugnis puts out a simple repast for which no one seems especially hungry, as it seems that tummies are already full of butterflies. Mal chats quietly with a few of his more trusted lords, and Nefarian is a restrained version of his usual gregarious self. At any rate, nobody's dragon bone chair gets dirty, which is, let's face it, your main concern.
    After breakfast, what will you do?

Visit the castle tailor, Bojanda, to make sure Mal's ceremonial garb is the picture of perfection?
Turn to 283.

Check in with Mrs Bleakheart, the head housekeeper, to ensure that all is ready for the final round of guests arriving today?
Turn to 16.

Or round up any idle hands to polish the castle's best tableware for the feast?
Turn to 176.

188

You take a look in the mirror, and a proud, proper butler stares back at you. That is what others must see too, if you are to make your escape from the castle without arousing suspicion.
    You decide to retain the garb of your station.
    You are DRESSED WELL.

Turn to 78.

189

'Behold,' shouts Mal, holding a hand out towards the path from which, any moment, the beast will emerge. 'The awesome ferocity of the zagga!'

The great roar turns suddenly to a pained yelp. There follows a muffled kerfuffle in the trees.

'What goes on?' asks Mal in annoyance. 'Mr Artanon! Go see what the matter is.'

You give a quick bow and, trying to maintain poise, hurry towards the path from the bestiary. You arrive to find a group of handlers pulling on the chains of an enormous, plaintively mewling zagga. It seems to be nursing a paw, which you realise with shock is bent the wrong way.

'Mr Artanon!'

Beastmaster Jhurgle approaches, his face white with worry.

'What has happened, Mr Jhurgle?'

'A loose stone on the path, of all the things. She took a tumble and now – doom help us – she's in no condition to complete the ceremony. She'll be too interested in licking her wounds and making a fuss.'

'Gods, sir, how could you let this happen? His Churlishness will not be happy ...'

'Please, Mr Artanon, barter me some time. I will fetch the backup beast with all possible haste!'

Note that you are ONE ZAGGA DOWN.

Jhurgle strides away shouting orders, leaving you as the unfortunate bearer of bad news.

Is the chosen zagga BLACK AND YELLOW?
Turn to 81.

Or RED AND GREEN?
Turn to 130.

190

'I am Rostolph,' you say, as you gently caress her buttocks.
You have told Rose A DANGEROUS LIE.

Turn to 258.

191

Although temptation stares you in the face - or maybe, to be more accurate, in the pants - you understand all too well what is at stake. The trouble you would cause by ruining the ceremony would in no way be worth any brief pleasure. Perhaps it has been too long between drinks, so to speak, but you are a man in control of his thirst.
 'Stygias will enjoy feasting on your soul,' you say.
 As you leave the dungeon, Roseblossom's weeping echoes off the walls.
 You to deliver the booze to the kitchen and head to bed.

Turn to 96.

192

You send for Jilly, with instructions to meet you on the level beneath the guest quarters. After leaving you dithering there a little longer than you would like, she arrives rather breathless.
 'Report,' you say.
 'I've done as you asked, Mr Artanon, though for

192 (cont'd)

the life of me I can't guess why.'

'Excellent. I have no doubt we will soon hear a ruckus.'

Sure enough, from the level above, you hear a door slam open, and exclamations of disgust.

'Come with me,' you tell Jilly, 'and play along'.

You lead her upstairs to the guest quarters, gliding along as if merely making some nightly rounds. You find both Rostolph and Nefarian standing outside their rooms in their bedclothes, Rostolph with a nasty circular bite mark on his arm.

'Is everything all right, sirs?' you ask, your face a mask of grave concern.

'No!' snaps Rostolph. 'This is simply not acceptable, Mr Artanon! Our beds are riddled with bedbugs! If it was only mine that would be one thing, but to find such vermin in Lord Nefarian's own quarters? What kind of household are you running, sir?'

You do a suitable job of looking horrified.

'By Stygias, my lord Nefarian,' you say, dropping to one knee and pulling Jilly down beside you, 'I offer more apologies than there are drops in the ocean. Forgive us for failing you so absolutely.'

'Come, come,' says Nefarian, slightly embarrassed by your drama, 'no need for all that. I'm sure these things happen from time to time. Just get it sorted out, will you? There's a good fellow.'

'Of course! Please, step into this guest chamber out of the draught,' you open a vacant room, 'while myself and Jilly here rid you of these intruders immediately.'

When the two of them are safely bundled away, you speak quietly to Jilly.

'Now, you clear the bugs from Nefarian's room, and I will do Rostolph's.'

She nods, and you each head to separate doors.

Upon entering Rostolph's room, you notice nothing immediately suspicious. There is a table, a bed, shelves, cupboards, and an adjoining door to Nefarian's quarters. Rostolph's travelling case is on the floor.

Where will you search for the poison?

Under the bed?
Turn to 206.

In Rostolph's case?
Turn to 164.

In the cupboard?
Turn to 132.

193

You reach the wall, which is covered by thick vines.

'Climb,' you tell Roseblossom.

She goes up first and you follow. It is a long climb, but the vines are thick and strong.

'Stay low,' you advise, as she reaches the top.

On the other side you start climbing downwards, some thirty paces to the ground.

Are you DRESSED PRACTICALLY?
Turn to 281.

Are you DRESSED WELL?
Turn to 149.

194

You move away from Haiken, whose hand still hovers uncertainly over the cutlery, to serve Mal rat heads. Finally Haiken makes a decision and picks up a carapace-cracking-spork.

Mal chuckles at his ignorance. 'By Stygias, Captain – have you been in the field so long that you've forgotten the basic functions of tableware?'

Haiken grimaces. 'Pardon me, your Pettiness. I may have had a noble birth, yet life as a soldier puts me out of touch with certain niceties. We tend to eat with our hands.'

Mal laughs. 'Well, let us not stand on ceremony, Captain! I am happy to do it your way!'

Mal picks up a rat head with his hand and shovels it into his mouth. Haiken happily follows suit, munching and cracking skulls with his teeth.

Inwardly, you give a sigh. No doubt with such messy fingers, Mal will stain the dragon bone. Why, you have often wondered, would anyone fashion a dining chair out of such easily blemished material as bleached porous bone?

Just as you fear, Mal leans back to rest his grubby mitts upon the armrests.

The CHAIR IS DIRTY.

You move back to the wall while your lords eat, to remain in waiting.

Turn to 18.

195

'My,' says Nefarian, 'it's a little on the nose in here! Are the realm's coffers so empty that you cannot afford cleaning staff, my lord?'

Mal is incensed by the insult, but even he may not strike out openly against Nefarian. Instead he turns to you with a nasty gleam in his eye.

'Mr Artanon,' he says loudly, 'you really should have ensured that everything was up to scratch.'

If MAL IS IRKED with you ...
Turn to 245.

If not ...
Turn to 178.

196

Feeling a slight twinge in your back, you bend over to resume watch through Rostolph's keyhole. Rostolph and Nefarian are at the table, while between them the tadpole swims about happily in its glass.

'... as you can see, my lord,' says Rostolph, 'the poison did not harm it. It would be a screaming giveaway if the cook served up a platter of dead tadpoles, but fortunately it looks like they're immune.'

'Mmm,' says Nefarian. 'Maybe. But I don't like it.'

'Lord?'

'You said the tadpoles are going to be the centrepiece dish. It will look extremely odd if I, and all my allies, refuse to partake of such a delicacy en masse.'

196 (cont'd)

'Ah ...'

'Honestly, this is not you at your conniving best.'

'I see what you mean, my lord.'

'We need a more specific dish - something Malacandros will gravitate towards when others will not.'

'Well, the cook did mention that he has a particular fondness for peas.'

'Peas? Yuck. Of all the horrendous things in the world, peas have got to be the worst.'

'You don't like peas, lord?'

'Nobody likes peas.'

'I think you'll find that some people quite like peas.'

'No, they don't. Peas are little abominations.'

'Um ...'

'Well done, Rostolph. We'll poison the peas.'

That old chestnut, eh, Mr Artanon?

It seems that Mal was quite right not to trust his cousin. Nefarian means to poison him at tomorrow's feast.   You have gained KNOWLEDGE OF FOUL PLAY. The question is, what are you going to do about it?

Go and tell Malacandros immediately?
Turn to 226.

Or do you prefer to sort these trifling matters out yourself, keeping background concerns like intended murder from spoiling your lord's special day? If so, think on what do do next while you go to check in at your office, as if everything was completely normal.
Turn to 142.

197

You pop open the bottle and waft the acidic stench of a fine Black Sav towards your nose. Pouring yourself a small glass, you tip it back and swirl the wine in your mouth. Beautiful notes of toxin hit your tongue, sharp without being overpowering.
    This is a lovely drop, and will do very nicely.
    Now, do you want to try:

The Sparkling *Bloodworm's Rest* Cabernet?
Turn to 111.

Nargletarg's Vineyard Dry Blue?
Turn to 224.

Glasscandle's Premium Scorpion Whisky?
Turn to 14.

Mrs Plugberry's Make-Me-Feel-Nice Cure-All Tonic and Tile Cleaner?
Turn to 87.

Or, if you are finished, pile up a cart full of booze and get out of here.
Turn to 168.

198

You follow a path through the trees and step out onto a rocky slope. Ahead, on the very edge of a sheer cliff, a twisted tower stands alone. On its flat roof you see the instruments of the skywatchers glinting – tubes pointing at the sky, strange oddments dangling from poles, a glass sphere on a

198 (cont'd)

pedestal, and various other bits and bobs. Figures move amongst them, making adjustments and taking readings.

'They predict a full moon three nights hence,' you say. 'They had better not be wrong, or Malacandros will be furious.'

Feralis gets a funny look.

'Are you all right, Mr Feralis?'

'Oh, yes, sir. It's just that ... well, the full moon is when my animal side becomes most difficult to control. I will crave to bound and hunt, yet I want to be on hand for the ceremony. I will have to ... contain my instincts.'

'Indeed. We will all have to be on our best behaviour for the ceremony, Mr Feralis.'

Feralis nods determinedly.

You are now privy to FERALIS'S WOES.

'We should leave the skywatchers to it,' he says. 'They are grumpy lot, and do not brook being disturbed with good grace.'

Would you like to head back to the clearing and then on towards the bestiary?
Turn to 136.

Or go and have a look at the castle's front gate?
Turn to 267.

Or go back to the castle?
Turn to 124.

199

You smile wanly and shake your head. 'Oh dear, Your Guilelessness. You've fallen for the oldest trick in the book.'

'What book?' growls Mal.

'You pointed me out to her. Do you really think a man of my character would be interested in some tanned young lady with unrestrained cleavage and smooth long legs?'

Mal glances at the girl uncertainly.

'You had your way with me!' she protests.

'Pish, tush. I'd rather poke my manhood into a box full of starving weasels, thank you very much. My lord, she has obviously heard my name bandied about, as I am rather omnipresent about the castle. Then you go and confirm my identity, so she can point at me even though she's never seen me before, making her story look more plausible. You know I would not usually speak so freely to you, my lord, but I must ensure you aren't made a fool of on this auspicious occasion.'

Mal frowns deeply, and rubs his chin. You can see that he is trying to believe you.

'She wants to live, oh Unwise One,' you say. 'Hence she will say anything.'

'How dare you!' Roseblossom screams. 'You liar! You ...'

'Silence,' says Mal, and her jaws snaps shut with some force. 'Let the ceremony continue.'

Are you aware of BLEAKHEART'S PREFERENCES?
Turn to 31.

If not, step back and let Mal continue.
Turn to 180.

200

You overtake the footmen along a corridor lit by stuttering candles, and lead them through a wide archway into the airy dining hall. Great windows stand open along one wall, looking out upon a pleasant view of circling lizard-birds cannibalising their young. Down the length of the hall runs an immense marble table, at the head of which the Dark Lord Malacandros reclines in a chair of elaborately carved dragon bone. He is a gaunt man with darting eyes and sharp features, currently dressed one of his best grey robes (which you helped him get into this morning), his black hair clasped in a ponytail down his back. To his right sits Captain Haiken, one of his favoured brutes, a well muscled orc in polished steel.

'Ah, Mr Artanon,' says Mal, 'I was beginning to worry we'd been forgotten.' He gives you a thin smile, which warns you he is very close to becoming irked.

You bow deeply. 'My humble apologies, oh Intolerant One. Repugnis is putting the final touches on today's main course, and you know what a perfectionist he is. In the meantime,' you whisk a platter from one of the footmen, 'here are some starters to whet your appetites.'

As you move toward the head of the table, Haiken licks his lips.

'Rat heads!' he exclaims. 'My favourite.'

Who will you serve first?

The enthusiastic Captain Haiken?
Turn to 45.

Or your master, Malacandros?
Turn to 113.

201

Mal's eyes narrow to slits. 'I thought I made my immediate desire for cheese fairly clear and present, did I not, Mr Artanon?'

You experience a sinking feeling. 'Yes, my lord.'

'Yet you have kept my guests and I waiting while you've been off, I don't know, catching butterflies and braiding their antennae?'

You decide not to point out how difficult and weird that would be.

'I encourage you do dally no further,' says Mal. 'Serve us!'

MAL IS IRKED with you.

Turn to 134.

202

'My lord,' you say, 'Miss Molsk was not really performing at the high standard we expect here at Cayfax Castle. I'm afraid I had to ... let her go.'

'Ah,' says Mal, 'that is a shame. I quite liked Molsk – she had a pleasant way about her.'

'Yes, my lord,' you say, although you can't imagine why even he would think such a thing.

'At any rate,' says Mal, 'I intended to have her consult with Mr Jhurgle today, and pick out the best zagga beast for the ceremony. Since you have dismissed her, I suppose you've inherited the task.'

With an inward sigh, you add the job to your long list of things to do. It seems you must find time to CONSULT WITH JHURGLE.

'Incoming!' calls a worker, and everyone turns to the stable doors in anticipation.

Turn to 103.

203

The good thing about chewing on dried meat is, it provides you with an ongoing snack as you pick bits out of your teeth on your way to your bedchamber.

Turn to 261.

204

You approach the keyhole, and bend over to peer through.

Rostolph's quarters adjoin his master's through an ornate door. You can also see a table laden with fruit, though Rostolph himself is not in view. A moment later he appears carrying a wooden box and a glass of water, and sits down. From the box he takes a jar containing what looks like red dust, then fishes in his pockets for the hanky-wrapped tadpole. He empties it out into the water, where it zips about madly, joyous to be returned to liquid.

Rostolph opens the jar and carefully taps some red dust into the glass of water. He then proceeds to watch the tadpole with a deepening frown.

Nothing seems to happen.

Are you WELL RESTED?
Turn to 117.

If not ...
Turn to 46.

205

Strike the note that says TIME FOR TWO THINGS. You now only have TIME FOR ONE THING.

Turn to 88.

206

Trying not to crumple the knees of your livery, you get down on all fours and look under the bed.

'Hello, Mr Artanon,' says Uther, the castle bogey man.

'Oh, hello Uther. Haven't seen you about for a while.'

'I've been hiding, as is my want. I was actually about to leap out and boo you until I realised who it was.'

'Well, I think you had better find another place to lurk. I'm not sure that these quarters are safe, even for an ethereal horror such as yourself.'

'Right y'are, sir.'

'Before you disappear, though, let me ask you this – have you overheard anything of note from this room's current occupant, a fellow called Rostolph?'

'Oh, I try not to listen, sir – respect for people's privacy, and all that.'

'Very good.'

'That said, while the gentlemen guest was making love to a scullery maid this afternoon – I was going to boo him too until I realised he had company – I did hear him mention how sad he was over his brother's recent execution. Sounded like he was playing the sympathy card to me, but still, it was interesting to hear that it was his own Lord Nefarian

who carried out the killing.'
'Really? Well, that is interesting.'
'He chuckled to himself after Little Miss Drops-Her-Pants departed, and added that he hated his brother, and is glad that he's dead. I suppose that explains why he's still happily serving Nefarian.'
'I suppose it does.'
'Anyway, I best be off. Boo to you, Mr Artanon.'
'Boo to you, Uther.'
The bogey-man fades away.
You now know about ROSTOLPH'S BROTHER.
Where will you search next?

In Rostolph's case?
Turn to 164.

In the cupboard?
Turn to 132.

207

You undress, and sorrowfully hang your livery up in the wardrobe. You know that you will probably never wear it again.
Where did it all go wrong?
Oh yes, when you had sex with that girl.
You put on some trousers and a loose shirt. You are DRESSED PRACTICALLY.

Turn to 78.

208

You hasten back to the dining chamber, hoping no one has missed you. At the entrance you snatch a tray of after-dinner mince from a footman, hoping to blend seamlessly back into the service. You circle the table scooping steaming mince onto plates, and eventually come to Mal.

'Ah, Mr Artanon,' he says. 'So good of you to join us. I was just asking after you, actually. You see, whilst everyone else had their servants on hand, it seems that I, the Dark Lord of All Nocturnia, was not being attended by my very own butler. Where, pray tell, were you?'

The calm, cold tone of Mal's voice scares you greatly. You can tell he is embarrassed to have been left wanting in front of so many important guests.

If MAL IS IRKED with you ...
Turn to 183.

If not ...
Turn to 257.

209

The zagga starts on the virgin's legs, snapping them like breadsticks. The arcane runes on the altar glow, redder than the blood which coats them. In the sky, Stygias opens his mouth and gives a satisfied moan that rumbles the very ground beneath your feet. A stench like a thousand corpses rotting in the mire wafts over you, and you know that you stand in the breath of a god.

'We honour you, Stygias!' Mal crows

triumphantly.

An unearthly voice booms down upon you, vibrating in your eardrums and fizzing in your sinuses.

'You have done well, Dark Lord Malacandros. May your reign be long and terrible.'

As the zagga nuzzles the last bits of sacrifice around the altar, Stygias seems to loom towards the ground. His great skull disintegrates to threads of vapour that swirl wildly through the awestruck crowd, then suck away into the obelisks around the edges of the clearing. The runes give a final pulse, and fade.

A cool breeze settles in, rustling around you like a quiet embrace. The accompanying silence is strange and electric, with everyone in quite a daze. Slowly, all look to Mal. When he notices their stares, he wipes his own stunned expression off his face.

'The ceremony is complete!' he announces, and the crowd explodes with rapturous applause.

You cannot help but feel relieved, although your night is far from over. As nobles spill forth to throw themselves at Mal's feet and declare their loyalty for all eternity, you begin to think about the arduous task ahead – of getting them all properly watered and fed.

Indeed, it is not long before, 'To the celebration feast!' declares Mal.

Turn to 271.

210

Your stomach is a burbling fondue that cannot be ignored. Why did you eat all that cheese before bed,

Mr Artanon, you great nincompoop? You sigh and sit up - you aren't going to get to sleep any time soon. Maybe a walk will settle your stomach?

You wrap your bedcloak around yourself and leave your room on your way to the dungeon – perhaps the screams of hapless prisoners will settle your tummy?

As you approach the sturdy dungeon door, however, Captain Haiken emerges and shuts it firmly behind him. When he sees you, he folds his arms in a very 'you shall not pass' kind of fashion.

If HAIKEN IS GRATEFUL ...
Turn to 131.

Otherwise, do you want to try continuing past him into the dungeon?
Turn to 82.

Or stop and say hello?
Turn to 56.

211

You go to sit in your office but, truth be told, as you open letters and glance over lists, you don't really take anything in. The castle is thick with expectation, to which you are not immune, and thus the hours drag by slowly. Even though plenty is going on, you have yourself been so well organised, there isn't much to do but oversee the cogs turning. Finally, after what seems like the better half of eternity, the darkening of evening comes.

You try not to hurry on your way to Mal's chamber – quicker steps do not quicken the moon –

211 (cont'd)

and find jittery honour guards waiting outside.

'Good evening, Mr Artanon,' says Captain Erkenslaw, the orc head guard, who never fails to impress with his excellent manners. 'May your life end in pain enough to recognise your own demise.'

'Thank you, Captain. And yours.'

'His Apallingness awaits within.'

You enter to find Mal in his underwear (black, of course), dithering over his ceremonial robe.

'Ah, Mr Artanon!' he says, and you can tell that he's a touch nervous. 'I think the robe will do nicely, don't you?'

'Yes, oh Apprehensive One. Let us get you into it, so that you can bask in your own glory.'

You are very careful as you dress Mal. You fluff the feathers at his shoulders and smooth the golden symbols that adorn his chest. You comb his hair and put it in a menacing ponytail, then on goes a magnificently oversized skull helm, with the fanged mouth open as if roaring (and allowing Mal to see).

'My shadow sceptre?' he asks, and you fetch him a knotted staff with a carved claw at the top gripping a crystal inside which dark forces swirl. Mal takes it and admires himself in the mirror.

'Fit to greet Stygias himself, my lord,' you say.

Mal smiles – now that he looks the part, his confidence has returned. 'Only one Dark Lord sees this night pass once every hundred years,' he says. 'Mine is a distinguished reign, wouldn't you say, Mr Artanon?'

'I often do, my lord.'

'Come, then. Let us repair to the ceremony site.'

Turn to 33.

212

'Kalag.'

You wave your subordinate over, and he is quick to attend. He is, after all, still quite nervous in your presence - which is only proper, of course.

'Look at this,' you say, pointing out the stain on the dragon bone armrest. 'It is imperative that you clean it off, leaving not a single trace behind.'

'Yes, sir,' says Kalag.

Despite his apparent attention, you notice that his eyes dart momentarily past your shoulder. Following his gaze, you see that a particularly shapely young maid has just entered the hall to help with the cleaning up.

Well, young men will be young men, you suppose – but you do not want Kalag distracted from this important task.

Are you an INTIMIDATOR?
Turn to 26.

Or a DIPLOMAT?
Turn to 249.

213

Lunch passes without incident, although you can't help but notice that Rostolph is conspicuously absent. The fact that Nefarian doesn't seem to care does nothing to calm your curiosity.

After lunch you head to the kitchen to get a meal of your own, and there you find your answer. Rostolph is being led about by Repugnis, who is pointing out various things enthusiastically.

'... the oven, as you can see, is of excellent

213 (cont'd)

bigness. I can fit a whole swamptrusker in there!'

'Impressive, Mr Repugnis.'

'And this is the spice cupboard ...'

You clear your throat. Rostolph turns to you with a thin smile ready on his face.

'Ah, Mr Artanon. So good to see you again.'

'I trust Repugnis is not boring you to tears, sir?'

'What?' says Repugnis. 'No, Mr Artanon, he ...'

'It was I who imposed upon Mr Repugnis to show me the kitchen,' says Rostolph. 'Lord Nefarian gets a funny tummy over certain foodstuffs, behooving me to check all menus and preparation areas. I'm happy to report that plenty in tomorrow's feast will agree with his constitution.'

'I am ecstatic to hear it.'

'I was just telling Mr Rostolph, sir,' Repugnis puts in, 'that we'll be serving Lord Malacandros' favourite dish – live balfrog tadpoles in fresh pond scum!'

You arch an eyebrow. 'Were you, indeed? That was very open of you, Repugnis. In all fairness, we should probably discover what Lord Nefarian's favourite dish is, and serve that also.'

Rostolph's smile widens. 'Oh, that won't be necessary, Mr Artanon, though you are very kind. I don't want to disrupt what Repugnis has planned.'

If you are a DIPLOMAT, you can choose to press the issue?
Turn to 138.

If you are an INTIMIDATOR, you can choose to *press* the issue?
Turn to 94.

Or you can tell Repugnis to continue with his tour of the kitchen?
Turn to 268.

214

Although the feast caters to all kinds of tastes, one dish is the clear standout – everybody wants to try a balfrog tadpole. The black little monsters squeak and hiss as they are popped into mouths, their protests crushed by chomping teeth.

'My word,' exclaims a fat noble, 'their bodies explode upon one's tongue with such putrid zest!'

'Ow! Yes, they certainly pack some bite.'

'You shall not pass,' says Mal with a grin, as he holds an angry tadpole between finger and thumb. 'Oh, no, wait a moment – you shall!' He pops the tadpole into his mouth with relish.

'Lovely,' says Nefarian, chewing on a still-wriggling tail. 'Though perhaps not quite as tasty as the peas, my lord – have you tried those yet?'

'Oh yes, I had them first. My favourite food, I don't mind telling you.'

'Ah, I had no idea. And how are you feeling, my lord? Quite well, I hope?'

Mal frowns at him. 'Yes, of course ...' He gets a strange look on his face, and suddenly clutches his chest. Nefarian's smile widens. 'Is there something wrong, Malacandros?'

'What ... have ... you ...'

'I certainly hope there wasn't some issue with the peas, my lord? Perhaps they have gone bad?'

Furiously, Mal tries to raise a hand to cast a spell at Nefarian, but his fingers spasm and his hands shake. Nefarian smiles smugly - an expression which, a moment later, freezes on his face. He gives a little cry, and clutches his own chest.

'My lord!' says Rostolph, rushing forward. 'Is everything all right?'

Are you BOUND TO NEFARIAN?
Turn to 38.

If not ...
Turn to 292.

215

Feralis's eyes light up madly. 'Kill?' he says, as the last glimmer of humanity leaves him. 'Death? Blood? Hunt? Slaughter?'

'These are not really questions per say, Mr Feralis.'

It seems you have not chosen your words wisely.

Feralis howls and bounds past you, knocking you from your feet. In a frenzy he pounces upon a noblewoman, and her brief screams are stifled as he wrenches out her throat. Blood arcs through the air and spatters across the altar.

The look on Mal's face turns to horror.

Turn to 284.

632

The fortune teller takes one look into her crystal ball, turns extremely pale, and bolts from her tent, leaving the door flapping in her wake.

You find yourself annoyed, Mr Artanon, as you have already paid your money up front. That's why you run after her, and, well, not to put too fine a point on it, you bloody well kill her.

So, what was that all about, eh? Mr Artanon?

216

First things first – say, for the sake of argument, that you do manage to access Rostolph's quarters and locate the poison. What will you then do with it?

Exchange it with a substitute, leaving Rostolph none the wiser?
Turn to 288.

Take the poison and leave a strongly worded anonymous note telling Rostolph that he and his lord had better tread carefully, for they are being watched?
Turn to 154.

Take the poison and leave a strongly worded *signed* note telling Rostolph that if he and his lord do not recompense you appropriately for the sensitive knowledge you now possess, you'll inform Malacandros of their plans?
Turn to 68.

If none of these choices seem appealing, you could go and serve dinner while considering better options.
Turn to 265.

217

You make your way to your quarters wondering how Peedy fared, and find the door partially ajar. Cautiously you open it, and are surprised to find Peedy sprawled on the floor with the jar of poison lying beside him. He looks up with watery eyes.
    'Mr ... Artanon ...'
    You go down on one knee. 'What happened?'

217 (cont'd)

'Strategically ... inserted spider hidden in ... Mr Rostolph's luggage, sir. Didn't affect me ... straight away. Mission ... successful.'

'What kind of spider?'

'Don't know. Green ... web.'

'Where did it bite you?'

Peedy turns his wrist to show you two little bite marks. Given your background in spider farming, you guess it must have been a hasp spider.

Your own spider, Bitey, hisses from the corner, and Peedy notices her for the first time. He gives a frightened yelp.

'Don't worry, Peedy. Bitey won't bite.'

'Can you ... help me ... Mr Artanon?'

'Yes, Peedy,' you say.

You pull your dagger from beneath your livery and slice open his throat.

'Believe me,' you tell him, as you search his pockets for your master key, 'this is a kinder way to go than the pain that's on the way.'

Peedy stares at you with disbelieving eyes, but it does not take long for the light to fade from them.

Strike PEEDY LIVES from your notes.

You go to the window and open it, then haul Peedy's corpse over and shove it out. He falls from view towards the crags below, where you hear a distant crunch. With any luck, lizard-birds will pick his body clean before dawn.

'Well done, Peedy,' you say, pocketing the jar of poison.

You now POSSESS POISON.

You soak up Peedy's blood with a couple of old hankies you were going to throw out anyway, then go to bed and drift off immediately into a deep and peaceful sleep.

Turn to 3.

218

Mal spins upon the dark priests.
 'Why aren't you chanting?' he shouts. 'Or something?'
 Hastily the priests start waving their daggers around and chanting as they circle the altar. The spectacle goes some way towards covering the uncomfortable break in proceedings. Mal attempts to maintain dignity, though you can tell he wants to cross his arms and tap his toe.
 'Posture, my lord,' you whisper. 'There are many eyes upon you.'
 'Thank you for reminding me, Mr Artanon. I had almost forgotten.'
 'My pleasure, oh Peevish One.'
 Suddenly a fresh roar sounds through the night, and you sigh with relief – another zagga is on the way. You send a silent prayer to Stygias asking that all loose cobblestones have been discovered, then feel a little worried about singling yourself out to him on this particular occasion.

Turn to 10.

219

'Come with me, Mr Rostolph.'
 You lead Rostolph towards the guest chambers, moving slowly enough for him to keep up while laden with luggage.
 'This is a marvellous castle, Mr Artanon,' he puffs. 'It must take a rare man to keep it presentable at all times.'
 'I like to think so, Mr Rostolph.'

219 (cont'd)

'I often think that lords have no idea how much work goes on behind their backs.'

'I'm sure they have more important things to worry about, Mr Rostolph.'

'Take Nefarian, for example,' continues Rostolph, notably excluding his master's title. 'Just between us, I bet he didn't think twice about packing so many frilly shirts and dragonclaw back scratchers, since it's muggins here who has to lug it. Can't be without his face powder and a choice of different hairbrushes for all of a couple of days, eh? And I warrant you could tell me similar tales.'

If Rostolph is trying to trick you into saying something denigrating about Mal, he is doing a pretty awful job of it. His contrived offhandedness aside - and the fact that Stygias knows who may be listening in the corridors of Cayfax Castle - but a butler, in your view, would always be the one to pack his master's hairbrushes, face powder, shirts and back scratchers.

Still, would you like to:

Play along and see where he's going with this, by confiding something about Mal in Rostolph?
Turn to 255.

If you are an INTIMIDATOR, you might like to put Rostolph firmly in his place?
Turn to 177.

Or if you are a DIPLOMAT, you could steer the conversation to less dangerous territory?
Turn to 86.

220

Looking at the animals in the pens, you wonder if you can help Mr Feralis with his problem.

'Mr Jhurgle,' you say, 'if I could divert from my primary purpose here for just a moment, I wonder if you'd consider putting an end to a concern of mine?'

'What did you have in mind, sir?'

'Mr Feralis has confided in me that he's worried about the full moon tomorrow night. As you are no doubt aware, it tends to exacerbate his werewolvian urges, and he fears being unable to concentrate at the ceremony if he does not satisfy them beforehand. I am thinking that if he had something to hunt in the early hours of the evening, perhaps ...'

You let your eyes wander back over the pens, and Jhurgle takes your meaning.

'Well,' he says, 'being dreadful friends with Mr Feralis myself, I'll certainly help him if I can. Would you like me to have a specimen boxed up and sent over to him before the ceremony?'

'That would be ideal, sir.'

'Very well. Certainly I can spare a briar beast or a fox, but which do you think is best? A fox is light and spry, and will lead Mr Feralis on a merry chase. The briars are comparatively slow and fat, but make up for that with armour and general viciousness.'

You consider the options.

Do you want to send Feralis a briar beast?
Turn to 173.

Or a fox?
Turn to 121.

Or find some better option later?
Turn to 280.

221

Servants move in an endless train clearing away tables and bringing fresh plates. All is jolly and well. The exceptions are Lord Nefarian and Rostolph, who you observe glancing from Mal's peas to Mal with a growing air of anticipation.

'Enjoying your peas, my lord?' asks Nefarian.

'Mmm-mmm!' says Mal. 'There's nothing finer than bowl of mushy peas! Would you like some?'

'Er ... no thank you, my lord. I am not as much a fan of the little green terrors as you.'

Suddenly Mal gets a strange look on his face, and clutches at his chest. He splutters and lurches out of his seat, knocking it backwards and shattering dragon bone all over the floor.

Nefarian's smile widens. 'Is something wrong, Malacandros?'

'What ... have ... you ...'

'I certainly hope there's not some issue with your peas, my lord? Perhaps they have gone bad?'

Furiously, Mal tries to cast a spell at Nefarian, but his fingers spasm and his hand shakes. His veins turn black and stand out from his skin. His face distorts with pain, and a moment later he pitches forward onto the table. White foam builds at the corners of his mouth, until he lies still.

Needless to say, the nobles are shocked.

'By Stygias!' exclaims Nefarian, rising to his feet. 'My dear cousin has apparently been murdered!' The look on his face turns from shock into a grin. 'By me!' he adds.

The nobles murmur and glance about. Some of them seem less surprised than others – in fact, some of them seem openly happy. Erkenslaw hovers by the door, his sword drawn, trying to work out what to do. He was loyal to Mal, but Mal is dead.

221 (cont'd)

'Haha!' says Nefarian, moving to the head of the table and pushing Mal's body aside. 'What a boorish fellow he was - that awful combination of vanity and insecurity. Not to mention his breath. You will find me, ladies and gentlemen, a much more *rewarding* Dark Lord. And while I realise some of you may have reservations about my timing, what with the ceremony and all that ... need I remind you that Stygias favours the strong? That he teaches us to follow our ambitions? Of course, if there are any here who object to my ascension ...'

Nefarian lets dark energy crackle through his fingers. His reputation as a powerful mage is known to all, and there are none, you warrant, who will dare to challenge him.

'... then I invite you to speak up.'

Erkenslaw glances at you, and you give a little shake of your head. He purses his rubbery lips, and slides his sword back into its sheath. As he stands down, the other guards relax.

The nobles, meanwhile, have survived too many successors to openly object to one such as Nefarian.

'All hail the Dark Lord!' calls a fat lord. He stands and raises his glass. Others are fast to follow suit, less they seem dangerously unenthused.

'Nefarian is the one truly blessed by Stygias!'
'This is *his* feast!'
'Praise Nefarian!'

Are you BOUND TO NEFARIAN?
Turn to 297.

Or are you CLUELESS?
Turn to 295.

If not ...
Turn to 294.

222

A group of footmen (feetman?) stagger into the dining hall under the weight of a large covered tray, supervised by Repugnis.

'Repugnis!' says Mal. 'I've just been telling the Captain what an excellent cook you are. I hope you don't force me to eat my words, haha.'

'I will not fail you, Malevolency,' says Repugnis. He clambers up onto the table, takes hold of the tray cover and, with an air of theatricality, whisks it away. A cloud of steam billows outwards, clearing to reveal a roasted briar beast.

'A precursor to the ceremony feast,' Repugnis announces. 'If my lord approves the dish, I can provide his guests with more.'

You scrape two carving knives together and shoo Repugnis off the table. As you set about carving the beast, Kalag dutifully appears by your side with plates at the ready. You pile them high with choice cuts of cheek, belly, and, of course, circles of stuffed intestine. Kalag delivers them to the lords, and all servants recede to anxiously await the outcome.

'Excellent!' proclaims Mal, and there is a collective wave of relief.

Turn to 101.

223

'Sarka?' he say gently, and she raises her head to look at you with watery, puppy-dog eyes.

'Forgive me, Mr Artanon,' she snuffles.

'What has reduced you to such a sorry state?'

Sarka looks embarrassed. 'Something the

servants said upset me. It shouldn't have, but, well – it's just that time of the month.'

'Oh,' you say, embarrassed. 'No need to share your personal women's workings with a stodgy old butler, Miss Sarka.'

Sarka giggles, which surprises you. 'No, Mr Artanon, I don't mean that. I was talking about the full moon.'

'Oh!' You are somewhat relieved. 'I see.'

'Yes. Every werewolf has heightened emotions around this time. It's the way of our folk.'

Are you privy to FERALIS'S WOES?
Turn to 161.

If not, why don't you give Sarka a scratch behind the ears, tell her not to worry, and head back to your office?
Turn to 211.

224

You've never had a great fondness for Blue, but as you sip *Nargletarg's*, you have to admit that the famous winemaker deserves his reputation. The wine has subtle tones of earth and decay behind the sour blue grapes from which it is made. One for a sophisticated palate, and certainly worth including.

Next, will you try:

The *Graveyard Pearl* Black Sauvignon?
Turn to 197.

The Sparkling *Bloodworm's Rest* Cabernet?
Turn to 111.

Glasscandle's Premium Scorpion Whisky?
Turn to 14.

Mrs Plugberry's Make-Me-Feel-Nice Cure-All Tonic and Tile Cleaner?
Turn to 87.

Or pile up a cart full of booze and get out of here?
Turn to 168.

225

Despite your misgivings, you give a globe a slow shake, and stare into its depths.

The snow swirls and forms into words, which sparkle and glow:

Detergent is not the only solution
to be found in the washroom.

You grimace, embarrassed to have even tried this silly toy, and push it away. The movement makes the words change.

You can't throw money at every problem, but
if your aim is true, you can hit a beggar
right between the eyes.

'Shush,' you tell the globe.
Discover the future in your own time, Mr Artanon.

Turn to 92.

226

You hasten to find Mal in the throne room. He is surrounded by sycophantic nobles, all bowing and scraping as they laugh at his jokes and tell him how wise and powerful he is.

It could be difficult to deliver quiet words to his ear.

Do you still attempt it?
Turn to 274.

Or do you decide these matters are really best left to an able-bodied butler? If so, think about what to do next on your way to check in at your office.
Turn to 142.

227

Roseblossom's eyes roll about wildly as she raises her head to search the crowd. You try to shrink into the other servants, but they are used to giving you plenty of berth, and keep on sidling away from you. It's a very annoying display of respect.

'The joke's upon you, Lord of Vileness!' Roseblossom screams. 'Should my blood touch this stone, you will earn the ire of your pestilent God!'

Mal stares down at her. 'Pardon me?'

'Just last night I spread my legs for man! I'm as much a virgin as your haggard old grandma!'

She laughs hysterically.

You can't see Mal's expression, but his voice seems to come from all directions at once, resonant in your ears for all its soft intensity.

'What did you say?'

227 (cont'd)

She looks Malacandros dead in the eye, as many have feared or failed to do. 'I am no use to you. I am impure.'

Mal is still for a long moment. He could extract the truth from her, you know that for a certainty, but he probably fears to do it here and now, as any spoilt blood that touches the altar will sully the ceremony and curse his reign.

'Who do you claim did this deed?' he asks. 'Tell me his name and I will let you go free.'

'I do not believe you, lord,' she says, 'yet I will tell you anyway, as I detest the thief for his cowardice.'

Mal touches her cheek in what could be mistaken for a tender gesture. 'Go on.'

You glance around, but with everyone frozen in fascination, any movement will be noticed. You may have missed your opportunity to flee, Mr Artanon.

Roseblossom throws back her head and shouts a name for all to hear.

What is it?

YOUR NAME?
Turn to 62.

A DANGEROUS LIE?
Turn to 28.

A SILLY ALIAS?
Turn to 37.

228

You know that despite, or maybe because of, their foul appearance, Harpies are actually quite vain creatures. Perhaps you should try a compliment – but what part of Molsk dare you single out?

Her feathers?
Turn to 22.

Her eyes?
Turn to 77.

Her smell?
Turn to 55.

Her claws?
Turn to 99.

229

You walk down the corridor feeling like you might have come this way before. As you reach the end, the only doorway available to you is on the left.

Go left?
Turn to 243.

230

'They will surely,' you add, 'remind everyone that you are not to be trifled with.'
    Mal considers himself in the mirror, swishing his tassels about.

'You can be quite dramatic at times, can't you, Mr Artanon?'

'Lord?'

'They are just tassels, after all.'

'On the spiky side, though.'

'Mmm.'

Once Mal is dressed, you excuse yourself and head to the kitchens to oversee breakfast preparations.

Turn to 187.

231

Sounds like it's time you checked in at your office.

You make the journey down to the servant's level and poke your head into a common room where staff socialise around a long table as they attend to various tasks. Along one wall is a bell array designed to summon servants to different sections of the castle.

Kalag sees you, puts down the waistcoat he has been mending, and leads everyone in a stand to attention.

'Back to work,' you say. 'I'm sure you've all got plenty to go on with. Sarka, is there mail?'

Sarka, a werewolf and general dogsbody, nods eagerly, flicking spittle from her lolling tongue. She's a little simple, and thus always pleased when she knows the answer to a question.

'Yessir – in your office, sir.'

'Very good.'

Satisfied that everyone is being productive, you retire to your office, where a desk surrounded by shelves stuffed with ledgers awaits you.

Would you like to look through your mail?
Turn to 170.

Or review your supply ledgers, in light of the fact that many guests will be entering the castle over the next few days?
Turn to 153.

Or, if PEEDY LIVES, you could choose to summon him.
Turn to 114.

232

You move closer to Mal and lower your voice.

'There is a servant who no one would miss,' you say. 'And I know for a fact she has never laid down with a man. Use her instead, and be assured of her purity. Technically speaking.'

'I did very much want to use a Brightlander,' Mal mutters in disappointment, 'but I suppose the rules don't expressly stipulate it. Who is this servant you mention?'

'Mrs Bleakheart, lord.'

'Oh, *that* sour-faced harridan. I don't care for her at all.'

'She is quite loathsome, my lord.'

'She doesn't react to any of my threats.'

'Mine either, lord.'

'Come to think of it, I'll be glad to be rid of her.'

Turn to 254.

233

Oh dear, Mr Artanon, it seems you got a little carried away with your sampling. You burp a multi-coloured burp and repress the urge to giggle a little. Admonishing yourself for your childish greed, you try to suppress how you feel and maintain decorum.
    Nonetheless, you are DRUNK.

Turn to 35.

234

You decide there are too many eyes peeking out of heads just now, and leave the poison in your pocket. At least you have stopped Rostolph using it!
    The FEAST IS FINE.

Turn to 262.

798

You reach into the back of the drawer, pushing aside this and that, when your finger brushes an unfamiliar object and sets it spinning. Curious, you draw it out into the candlelight.
    It is egg-shaped, and covered with a crinkly substance that is somewhat metallic and yet yields to gentle pressure. Tearing back some of this 'wrapping', you discover that the egg inside is a deep chocolatey brown. You give it a sniff, and discover that it IS indeed chocolate!
    What manner of egg is this, Mr Artanon?

235

With one aspect of your plan locked in, it's time to work out the more difficult part. How are you going to get into Rostolph's quarters?

Simply go and use your own master key to let yourself in while everyone is at dinner? You may be missed, though with plenty of other servants on hand, hopefully not.
Turn to 106.

Perhaps you have some KNOWLEDGE OF BEDBUGS which might prove useful?
Turn to 74.

If PEEDY LIVES, he certainly owes you a favour – you could give him your key and send him in your place!
Turn to 137.

236

'If you are rushing things at the last moment, Mrs Bleakheart,' you say, 'when you have known the precise day of the ceremony for months, then your singular lack of preparation so astounds me, that I might just *organise* these molten bed sheets into some kind of makeshift noose, to go around that rubbery neck of yours.'

Bleakheart stares at you, then gives a slow shrug. 'In which case we'll be even more short-staffed, Mr Artanon.'

You cannot help but sigh. 'Would you like me to send you some extra help, Mrs Bleakheart?'

'That would be most useful, Mr Artanon, now that I come to think of it.'

You leave the cloudy chamber, seize a passing servant, and order him to round up some dogsbodies for Mrs Bleakheart.

Turn to 211.

237

You enter your quarters thinking about what you might need for the journey ahead. You pack a small bag (you want to travel light) with garments that do not scream 'butler-on-the-run', and all of your savings.

You find yourself wondering if you should change out of your livery. Folk around the castle are used to seeing you in it, so leaving it on could be the best way to avoid attention. However, it may prove impractical for running, jumping, climbing, and other fleeing-related activities.

If you put on some regular clothes ...
Turn to 207.

If you leave on your livery ...
Turn to 188.

238

Repugnis looks at you in a way which, if you didn't know he wouldn't dare, you might find slightly accusatory.

'Mr Artanon,' he says, 'don't you recall polishing

off pretty much our entire cheese supply late last night?'

The memory of your greediness makes you sweat lactose.

Have you ENSURED ADEQUATE CHEESE SUPPLY?
Turn to 165.

Otherwise ...
Turn to 140.

239

Nefarian pitches forward onto the table. He shudders a little, then lies still. Hesitantly, Mal pokes him with a fork.

'Nefarian is dead!' Mal exclaims in joyous amazement. It is short-lived, however, for the stares of the nobles collect upon him. Nefarian was influential, with lots of powerful allies - who, if united, could prove a formidable opposition to Mal, a fact which is not lost upon him.

He tries to exorcise elation from his voice. 'Who in Nocturnia would do such a thing?' he asks, his sudden affront not overly convincing. 'They will be punished! Quite badly! Nefarian was my very blood relation, after all!'

Mal is in need of a scapegoat, and you think you have just the candidate.

You clear your throat. 'My lord,' you say, 'it behoves me to tell you that ... the butler did it!'

'You?' Mal says, in disbelief.

'Not I,' you say, 'but the *evil*, evil butler.' You point at Rostolph. 'Mr Rostolph, my lord! I have observed him in possession of poison, and he had unhindered access to the feast. He also would have known his lord's favourite food, which I myself had no idea was eel terrine.'

'Me?' The colour drains from Rostolph's face, yet he still manages to sound incredulous. 'Why would I murder my own employer? Such action is akin to stabbing oneself in the foot!' He sticks his chin out defiantly. 'I say, sir, that those who point fingers are most likely covering their own guilt. I say it was you who did this deed, Mr Artanon!'

All eyes turn to you.

Do you know about ROSTOLPH'S BROTHER?
Turn to 300.

If not ...
Turn to 299.

240

'I would like to have a look at the ceremony site, Mr Feralis.'

'Of course, sir. Going to be a very important occasion, after all.'

Feralis leads you through the grounds to a large plateau on which there stands a wood of grey trees. You walk between them and emerge into a perfectly circular clearing ringed by obelisks, in the middle of which is a stone altar covered in mystical symbols.

'We've clipped the branches and trimmed the grass,' says Feralis. 'There were some weeds growing around the obelisks, but they're beheaded now, sir, you can be sure of that.' You detect a hint of pride in his voice. You have to admit that the site does seem well maintained.

'You are a credit to the castle, Mr Feralis,' you say, and he gives you a very toothy smile.

'Thank you, sir.'

There are some other pathways leading out of the clearing, one to the bestiary and one to the skywatcher's tower.

Would you like to head in the direction of the bestiary?
Turn to 136.

Or towards the skywatcher's tower?
Turn 198.

Or leave Feralis and go back into the castle?
Turn to 124.

241

With the kitchen tour all wrapped up, you order Repugnis back to work.

'Just one more request before I go, Mr Artanon,' says Rostolph. 'I wonder if I may be so bold as to taste-test a balfrog tadpole or two - purely for my own edification, you understand.'

His request is indeed unusually forward. Should a butler be allowed to try an exquisite dish before his master?

Will you allow this?
Turn to 162.

Or not?
Turn to 289.

242

You follow the sound of werewolf whimpering, and discover Sarka hunched in an alcove.

Are you an INTIMIDATOR?
Turn to 291.

Or a DIPLOMAT?
Turn to 223.

243

You walk down the corridor feeling like you might have come this way before. As you reach the end, the only doorway available to you is on the left.

Go left?
Turn to 229.

244

You while the afternoon away with supply requests, bills, applications, complaints, and various other bits and pieces. Nothing taxing, which gives you an opportunity to reflect on all that has been going on.
　　As the afternoon begins to wane, there comes a knock at the door.
　　'Enter.'
　　Sarka peeks in, carrying a package, which she holds tentatively, as if it contains a live snake.
　　'Mr Artanon, this just arrived. It's addressed to Ms Podger. I, er ... well ...'
　　'It's all right, Sarka. Leave it with me.'

Sarka puts the package down with some relief and leaves. You pick it up and turn it in your hands. Ms Podger was a pleasant young lady who, until recently, worked in the dining hall. Unfortunately she dripped a spot of gravy on Mal's arm, so he had hers ripped off and used to strangle her.

She therefore has little use for whatever this may be.

Do you wish to open it?
Turn to 21.

Or readdress it to her family and have it sent onwards?
Turn to 266.

245

Without being able to take out his frustration on Nefarian directly, Mal needs to assuage his embarrassment in front of the nobles by finding someone else to make a show of holding responsible. Knowing this provides you with a little comfort as he conjures shadowy claws from the ground and pull you down to strangle the life out of you.

But not much.

Your service ends here.

246

The red and green zagga growls and lowers her dripping maw to the sacrifice, who shrieks long and hard. Mal laughs, and the crowd echoes him.

In the sky, the skull's eyes blaze and rake the altar with yellow beams.

'Devour her!' Mal shouts. 'Tear her apart!'

The zagga sniffs at the sacrifice. She wrinkles her nose, gives an unethused growl, and twitches her ears. Then she rocks back on her haunches and starts to preen.

Uneasy muttering breaks out.

'What's wrong with it?' Mal demands of Jhurgle.

'I ... ah ... maybe she isn't hungry?'

'Why isn't it hungry? I thought you were starving them.'

'Er ...' says Jhurgle. 'I, er ... maybe she found a snack somewhere?'

'A *snack*?' Mal is livid. 'I will make a snack out of ...'

He trails off as he notices that the skull in the sky seems to have loomed closer, to focus upon him directly.

'Just one moment, oh Magnificent Stygias!' cries Mal. 'We will ... be with you shortly.' He lowers his voice and hisses at Jhurgle. 'Is there another zagga?'

Are you ONE ZAGGA DOWN?
Turn to 284.

If not ...
Turn to 163.

247

'That is very flattering, Mr Artanon,' says Rostolph, seeming genuinely pleased. You can only assume the balding runt receives few compliments on his appearance. 'These garments are made from bellspider silk, all the way from the southern ranges.'

'Ah, yes - I know a thing or two about spider silk, Mr Rostolph.'

'Oh?'

'My father was a spider farmer, you see.'

'You don't say.'

'He often dreamt of rearing bellspider stock, but the climate of our homestead would never have supported them. Mostly we trafficked in malodorous greenbacks ...'

You settle in to a nice old chat about the different kinds of spiders and different kinds of silk. It seems you both share quite a passion for fine clothing. In fact, you have to admit, you quite enjoy talking to a like-minded chap about such things, as opportunities are rare.

If you have not already BONDED WITH ROSTOLPH, you have now.

At the doorway, Lord Nefarian clears his throat.

'I hope I'm not interrupting anything?' he says calmly, entering.

Turn to 108.

248

You find your eyes wandering over the curves of Roseblossom's body, your clouded mind whispering that *this is a good idea at the time.* It has been a while, hasn't it, Mr Artanon? What better respite from the burdens of duty than a dalliance with a pretty young virgin?

Fumbling slightly, you put your master key in the lock – a harbinger of things to come? – and Roseblossom withdraws to lean against the back wall. As you approach she begins to hike her skirt up her thighs, and all hope of sense abandons you as you realise she wears nothing to protect her nethers.

'I would know the name of my saviour,' she

whispers, shrugging off the shoulders of her dress.
What name will you give her?

Your own?
Turn to 276.

A silly alias?
Turn to 135.

Or will you make up a dangerous lie?
Turn to 190.

249

'Ah, my boy,' you say, lowering your voice to conspiratorial tones, 'could it be that you fancy that lovely young lady?'

Kalag blushes. 'I'm sorry, sir. I did not mean to be so obvious.'

'Well, these things are to be expected when the sexes work in close proximity. But need I remind you that true professionals do not fraternise in the workplace?'

'No, sir.'

'Save that for your off-hours, when your time is your own.'

'Yes, sir. Of course, sir.'

'In the meanwhile, put your ardour into cleaning his Awfulness's chair, yes?'

Kalag nods and, satisfied he will do a good job, you leave the hall.

You have TRUSTED IN OTHERS.

You also have TIME FOR TWO THINGS before you need to check in at your office.

Turn to 88.

250

Molsk drops lightly out of the air.

'Here I am, your Maniacalness.'

As she splays her wings before the dark lord, she wafts her fetid body odour over you both, and you gulp down the bile rising in your throat.

'Ah,' says Mal, 'there you are, Stinkfeathers.'

Molsk's scaly cheeks turn a darker shade of grey, and it takes you a moment to realise she is blushing. As you glance between her and Mal, unwelcome thoughts encourage the bile on its upward journey.

'I have a task for you,' says Mal. 'I want you to consult with Mr Jhurgle and choose the best zagga beast we have for the ceremony.'

'Of course, my lord,' says Molsk, bowing low.

Make a note that Molsk will select the BLACK AND YELLOW ZAGGA.

'Incoming!' calls a worker, and all turn to the stable doors in anticipation.

Turn to 103.

251

You clear your throat very slightly, and Haiken glances up at you. As you move your hand back from his plate, you let your finger rest momentarily on the appropriate rat-head-eating fork. Haiken understands, and gives you a relieved look.

Mal is too busy shovelling slug meat into his gullet to notice the exchange, so HAIKEN IS GRATEFUL.

You add some rat heads to Mal's plate and move back from the table to take a place in waiting.

Turn to 18.

252

'Mr Feralis,' you say, surreptitiously reaching to your belt where the dagger is hidden, 'if I could impinge upon you to step aside for a moment ...'

Warily Feralis lets you take his shoulder, while casting a glance back at the quivering Roseblossom.

'Now,' you say, 'allow me to explain ...'

You draw the dagger and plunge it at his chest, but his wolfish reflexes kick in and he springs back snarling. You lunge again, but he's too fast. He dodges your blow and pounces, driving you to the ground and knocking the air from your lungs. You try to gasp out, but unfortunately his instincts have taken over. He clamps down on your throat, and rips out your wind-pipe.

To think, after so many years of excellent service, that this is how you will be remembered.

253

'Lord Malacandros,' you tell Jhurgle, 'has asked me to consult with you about choosing an appropriate zagga for the ceremony.'

'Ah! Come then, I shall have them dragged out of their dens for inspection.'

You make your way out the back of the bestiary into a kind of amphitheatre, where tiered seating overlooks an earthen pit with a portcullis gate set in the side. The gate opens and a team of handlers pull two zaggas out, secured by multiple chains. They are sizeable creatures with fang-filled mouths, easily capable of chomping a man in a couple of bites. They have round faces with huge black eyes, their nostrils buried under the long fur that covers them from

253 (cont'd)

head to toe in remarkable coloured bands – the larger one red and green, the smaller black and yellow.

'We've been deliberately starving these two,' says Jhurgle, 'as zaggas actually subsist for quite a few days between meals. We don't want their appetites ruined before they nosh on virgin, eh? So, which one do you think?'

'I must admit,' you say, 'that when His Thoughtlessness assigned me this task, I felt a little out of my depth. What would be your criteria for selection?'

Jhurgle frowns. 'I suppose the size of the red is worth a mention, though all zaggas are equally ferocious. She is also older and more wily, while the yellow is younger and harder to control – more wilful, more bloodthirsty.'

You are still a bit confounded, and it does not help that the pressure is great to make the right choice.

'I may defer to you in this instance, Mr Jhurgle. Which one would you pick?'

'Call me a simple man, but a larger beast seems appropriate on such a grandiose occasion.'

It's up to you, Mr Artanon. Choose either the RED AND GREEN ZAGGA or the BLACK AND YELLOW ZAGGA, and note which one.

You bid farewell to Mr Jhurgle and head back to the castle.

Turn to 92.

254

'Seize Mrs Bleakheart!' Mal commands Erkenslaw.

Bleakheart, who stands with the servants, removes her pipe from her mouth in surprise. 'What?'

'Do it!'

With some trepidation the orc captain moves towards Bleakheart, waving for his guards to join him.

'Watch her,' warns Erkenslaw. 'She's got a mean left hook.'

'Now you look here,' says Bleakheart. 'I do not ...'

'Now!'

Erkenslaw leaps on Bleakheart, wresting her to the ground with the help of his guards.

'Bring her to the altar!' says Mal. 'And take the Brightlander away!'

Bleakheart puts up quite a struggle, until Erkenslaw thumps her on the head with the pommel of his sword. The blow is too light to spill any blood, yet enough to make her groggy.

'That's for breaking my wrist,' you hear him say.

Before you know it, Mrs Bleakheart is being strapped to the altar.

'And *now*,' Mal says gleefully, 'let's get on with it!'

The crowd cheers.

You may strike DEFLOWERED THE VIRGIN from your notes.

Turn to 180.

255

You slip back to walk alongside Rostolph, while giving a woe-is-me-style exclamation of agreement.

'It is the way of things, it seems,' you say. 'Malacandros is equally hopeless – he'd piss on his own rug til grass grew out of it, if someone wasn't leaving him a fresh chamberpot every day.'

'Ha!'

'And when he lifts his arms to be fitted for a robe ... well, it wouldn't hurt him to scrub his pits once a year, let that be said.'

Rostolph chuckles and gives you an appraising sidelong glance, which you catch in your own peripheral vision.

'I shouldn't complain too much about Lord Nefarian, however,' he says. 'He's generally quite easy to look after. And he pays his loyal servants very well. *Very* well indeed.'

'Oh?'

'Last year he gave me a bonus bag of onyx at Darktide, simply because he was happy with my work.'

'How magnanimous.'

'It spent very well, I can assure you.'

You wonder where all this is leading.

'Here,' you say, taking a bag from Rostolph, 'let me help you with that.'

'Thank you, sir – you are too kind.'

Could it be that you have BONDED WITH ROSTOLPH? Perhaps, perhaps not, but make a note of the state for now.

Turn to 52.

256

'Ho, good fellow,' you say, approaching the guard, who peers at you with piggy eyes from under his helm.

'Mr Butler,' he grunts.

'I must, er, inspect the dungeon.'

The guard frowns suspiciously.

'Lord Malacandros wants to take Lord Nefarian on a tour of it tomorrow,' you clarify. 'I have to ensure it is horrible enough to meet his exacting standards. We wouldn't want the Dark Lord unhappy with us, would we?'

This convinces the guard. He unlocks the door and opens it for you. As you enter the dungeon, you give a contrived exclamation of surprise.

'What is it?'

'One of the prisoners is out of his cell!'

'What?' The guard blusters past you. 'Where? I'll string them up by their ...'

You slip your dagger through a join in his armour into his back.

'Urk!'

The guard staggers forward, trying to draw his sword – orcs are tough, and thick skinned – but you hammer the blade in deeper with the flat of your palm, and hear the sound of his spine crunch.

He falls to the floor.

With some effort you drag his corpse into an empty cell, praying no one hears his armour scraping loudly along the ground.

Turn to 110.

257

'Forgive me, oh Deprived One,' you say. 'I was attending to various requirements for the ceremony tomorrow. I know you will want everything to be just so.'

You notice that Rostolph, standing behind Nefarian, is eyeing you curiously.

'Well,' says Mal, 'you should have looked after all that at some other time. If there are any further absences from you, Mr Artanon, they may tend to prove enduring. Do I make myself clear?'

'As a cloudless night, my lord.'

'Good. Now take this horrendously sullied napkin off my lap and prepare the drawing chamber for brandy and cigars.'

MAL IS IRKED with you.

Turn to 70.

258

You spare a thought for your spider-silk pants as they drop to the floor, but it is the briefest thought humanly possible for a person to have.

Roseblossom guides your gentlemanhood into place with her hand and, from the resulting reception and arcing of her back, coupled with her throaty moans and eager lips, you would swear she's not really a virgin at all.

You proceed to have a very good time indeed, Mr Artanon, you old dog.

You have DEFLOWERED THE VIRGIN.

An efficiently spent amount of time later, you pull your pants up, and brush off roach legs and fragments of bone. The clarity of release brings with it the staggering implications of your actions, during which the only thing you failed to discharge was your duty.

You cannot believe you have been so reckless! It is completely out of character - almost as if someone else was making your choices for you, just for a bit of cheap titillation.

'If you will only spirit me away from here,' whispers Roseblossom, her palm soft on your cheek, 'I promise to be yours, to do with as you choose, for however long you want. Please, sir – they're going to murder me.'

Her beautiful blue eyes fill with tears.
What say you, 'sir'?

'I shall do my best to free you, but we're going to need supplies. I'll return within the hour, sweet Roseblossom.'
Turn to 4.

'Get away from me, Brightlander harlot – you've caused me enough trouble as it is. I look forward to seeing Stygias consume your soul.'
Turn to 290.

259

You drag a goblin maid to the chair and point out the dirty armrest.

'You see this stain here?'

'Yessir, Mr Artanon,' she gibbers, her out-of-sync eyeballs rolling independently between you and the chair.

'It is very important that you clean it off. Do you

understand?'
 'Yessir, sir, yessir.'
 'Repeat what I've just told you then, you mindless excuse for a piece of shit.'
 'You want the, er, the stain cleaned off the chair, sir.'
 You take her by the shoulders and give her a good hard shake, snapping her head back and forth to see if that's all it takes to wipe her memory.
 'Now,' you say, 'tell me again.'
 The goblin frowns, trying to form thoughts in her jostled mind. 'Er ... you want ... yessir ... you want ... the stain cleaned off the chair, sir!'
 'That's right.'
 Satisfied that the goblin has retained your instruction, you leave her to take care of it.
 You have TRUSTED IN OTHERS.
 You also have TIME FOR TWO THINGS before you need to check in at your office.

Turn to 88.

260

'Heightened emotions, eh?' you say. 'From what I understand of werewolves, all desires burn hot under the light of the full moon. To hunt, to kill ... to mate.'
 If you could see beneath her fur, you would swear Sarka was blushing.
 'It's true, sir.'
 'If you were to satisfy one urge,' you say, 'would it go some way towards sating the others?'
 'It may ... sir.'
 'Ahem. Well, given that I need complete focus from my staff, I wonder if perhaps I should order

you to find the time, between now and midnight, to pay a visit to Mr Feralis? Perhaps you can even discover a mutual solution to your shared problem?'

Sarka blinks at you with big brown eyes. 'Mr Feralis? But he is such a handsome wolf.'

'A handsome wolf struggling to contain a building tension,' you say. 'Liable to frenzy at the slightest provocation.'

Sarka's eyes sparkle. 'Well,' she says, a little breathlessly, 'if you don't mind, sir, I might well try and be somewhere around Mr Feralis when the moon rises.'

'Excellent. In the meantime, back to scrubbing teapots with you.'

'Yes, sir. Thank you, sir.'

You watch her scurry off, satisfied that you have put THE SARKA SOLUTION into effect.

Turn to 211.

261

You enter your bedchamber, which lavishly befits your position in the castle hierarchy. A four poster bed stands in the middle the room, a plush green rug covers the cold stone of the floor, and your pet spider Bitey hisses at you from her web up in the corner of your well-stocked bookshelf (Bitey is a low maintenance pet who serves as a reminder of your family roots, and therefore the path which you deftly avoided).

Tired from the day's exertions, you put on a thick, comfy bedcloak and ease into bed. Surely, sleep will come swiftly.

Have you EATEN A LOT OF CHEESE?
Turn to 210.

If you have not done anything quite so foolish just before bedtime ...
Turn to 90.

262

Kalag enters the kitchen. 'Sir,' he says, 'the speeches are over – they are ready for the mains.'
　'Take them up.'
　Rostolph pushes his way into a line of footmen who stand waiting to be assigned their dishes.
　'If you'll excuse me,' he says, picking up a bowl of steamed cauliflower, 'this is one of Lord Nefarian's favourites, so I want to make it gets put near him. But, let me see, I am not yet taxed beyond carrying capacity. I could also take ...' He makes a show of looking around at other dishes. 'Ah! This will balance perfectly in my other hand.' He picks up a bowl of peas.
　His little performance is wasted on the group, for Repugnis is fussing about getting the most able-bodied carriers on the tadpole tureen.
　Food starts heading out the door.

Turn to 15.

263

Rostolph turns white.
　'Excuse me, sir?'
　'I saw you take that nibbler out of your mouth,

Mr Rostolph. What are you playing at?'

'Oh ... I, er, yes. I suppose it does seem like strange behaviour. I can assure you that I simply, er ... I have a keen interest in the study of amphibians, you see. I wanted a live sample to add to my collection, that's all.'

'You could have just asked.'

A cloud of distrust hangs between you. If you were BONDED WITH ROSTOLPH, that is no longer the case.

Suddenly Rostolph bows, and you turn around to see Lord Nefarian standing in the doorway.

'I hope I'm not interrupting anything?' he says calmly, entering.

Turn to 108.

264

Feralis gets a deranged look in his eye. 'Sniff?' he says.

'Yes, Mr Feralis, sniff indeed. Something is stumbling around out there, all alone in the dark. Maybe even a guest who is running late to the ceremony?'

The last traces of humanity drain from Feralis. Without another word he bounds off between the trees to hunt down this imaginary prospect.

You breath a sigh of relief.

Turn to 42.

265

You enter the dining chamber carrying a tray of lizard tartlets, and tong them onto guest's plates before taking up position behind Mal. Nearby Rostolph waits on Nefarian, though there is little communication, non-verbal or otherwise, going on between them as the meal passes. The guests gorge themselves until they bulge at the stitches.

'Time for brandy and cigars!' Mal announces. 'Let us adjourn to the drawing chamber.'

Turn to 70.

266

You look up Ms Podger's file and discover her closest living relative to be her mother, with an address in the poorest part of Cayfax Town. Perhaps the contents of this package will bring the woman some respite from the fact her daughter was brutally murdered for very little reason?

You readdress the package and put it with your outgoing mail.

Good man, Mr Artanon.
Turn to 92.

267

You and Mr Feralis make your way down pathways towards the spiky wall that jaggedly rings the entire mountaintop. The cobblestones underfoot are well polished, the grass to either side is closely shaved, and patrolling guards stand to attention as you pass. As you reach the front gate itself, you see that the portcullis is lowered, but only because it is being cleaned of rust by a troop of industrious workers.

'Everything looks fine to me, Mr Feralis,' you say. 'We have no cause for shame from guests arriving this way.'

'Thank you, sir.'

Do you now want to go and inspect the ceremony site?
Turn to 240.

Or head back into the castle?
Turn to 124.

268

'Please,' you say, 'I have interrupted – continue showing our guest around the kitchen, Mr Repugnis. I will join you, and enjoy rediscovering wonder in familiar things through new eyes.'

Repugnis nods and beetles off, leaving Rostolph little choice but to follow.

'And here,' says Repugnis, stopping in front of a row of glass tanks, one of which is teeming with balfrog tadpoles, 'is the centrepiece to be. We are keeping them well fed on bread crumbs so they don't eat each other. Also they will be nice and full when consumed, sort of a self-stuffing mechanism.'

'Delectable,' says Rostolph.

In the next tank is a large eel, coiled sleepily around a rock.

'What about this fellow?' says Rostolph.

'Hmm? Oh, that's just my pet, Eelliot.'

'Ah, a shame. My master does enjoy a nice eel terrine.'

'Well he shall have one,' you say. 'Repugnis, make sure there is eel terrine for Lord Nefarian.'

'But ... er ...' Repugnis glances into the tank. 'I don't have any fresh eels besides Eelliot here ...'

'Really,' Rostolph says, 'it's no trouble, Mr Artanon.'

'Nonsense! Repugnis can always find another pet. Consider it a sacrifice of your own, Repugnis, to echo that which takes place in the ceremony. Do you happen to know if Eelliot is a virgin?'

'He is, sir,' says Repugnis miserably. 'I raised him from a speck, and he's had no company but me.'

'Well, quite fitting then, don't you agree?'

'Yes, Mr Artanon, sir.'

Turn to 241.

269

You feel quite uncomfortable standing in Rostolph's quarters while Nefarian behaves in such a familiar manner.

'Please, Mr Artanon, have a seat,' he says. 'Rostolph, be a terrible chap and fetch us some tea.'

You have little choice but to do as he says.

'I must thank you, lord,' you say. 'I can't help but feel that you interceded on my behalf earlier today.'

'Oh, pish and tush, Mr Artanon. I know a valuable man when I see one, and my cousin can be a little reckless when it comes to executing people on the spot for no reason. It's a practice which I frown upon, if only from behind closed doors.'

He gives you a wink.

Rostolph joins you at the table with some cold

269 (cont'd)

cups of tea.

'One or two?' he asks, reaching for the salt bowl.

'Just one, thank you.'

'So,' says Nefarian, 'Rostolph tells me you have become fast friends.'

'We have a job in common, my lord, though I'm sure our discussions on butlering would bore you senseless.'

'Oh, I don't know - I like to make sure my people are happy. Fulfilled workers are dutiful workers, I always say. Why, if I was Dark Lord, there would be some changes in management style around here, I can promise you that.'

Nefarian is very casual about making this treasonous remark, then watches you closely for your response.

You decide you had better tread very carefully.

'Lords come and go,' you say, 'but a butler will always buttle.'

Nefarian laughs, and gives Rostolph a little nod. 'Rostolph may have mentioned that I am generous with my loyal servants.'

Rostolph places a cloth bag on the table and lets onyx coins slide out of it.

'I'm sure it will come as no surprise to you, Mr Artanon,' continues Nefarian, 'as it has always been the way of our people ... but say that I have ambitions to advance myself in Nocturnia's hierarchy? Ambitions which require a certain current title holder to be caught unawares by some grave misfortune? In such circumstances, I wonder ...'

He waves absently at the bag of coins.

'... if these coins may prove heavier than any weight upon your conscience, and tip the scales in favour of you siding with me?'

What a difficult position, Mr Artanon. It is obvious

that these tricksters have some kind of plot against your master, and you very much doubt refusal to play along will get you out of this room alive.
    Nevertheless, do you say:

'What would you have me do, my lord?'
Turn to 171

'Respectfully, I could never betray the rightful Dark Lord, Malacandros.'
Turn to 179.

270

As you present the berries and meat to Mal, you try to be discreetly small-voiced.
    'Words cannot convey the enormity of my remorse, your Captiousness, but I'm afraid, due to a catastrophic oversight, that the kitchen has run out of cheese.'
    Mal's face twists with rage.
    'The issue,' you continue hastily, 'is fast being remedied, oh Fastidious One. In the meantime, Repugnis assures me these berries are the plumpest in the land, and these strips of meat drier than tomb dust.'

If MAL IS IRKED with you, and you are IN NEFARIAN'S DEBT ...
Turn to 63.

If MAL IS IRKED with you ...
Turn to 89.

Otherwise ...
Turn to 155.

271

You track down your staff amongst the crowd, who are chatting excitedly about what they have just experienced.

'Mr Kalag,' you say, 'round everyone up and get back to the castle. I'll join you as soon as his lordship is situated in the dining hall.'

Truth be told you would rather go with him, to make sure preparations are properly underway, but you dare not leave Mal alone wearing such complicated attire - thus you hover while he speaks with unctuous stragglers.

'A convincing show, oh Legitimate One,' says Nefarian. 'There's no doubt that your greatness is cemented, if there ever was.'

Mal gives a confident smile – perhaps he no longer feels threatened by Nefarian?

'Thank you, cousin. You may take a place beside me at the feast, if you like. I imagine it must be quite a thrill, to experience such proximity to real power.'

'Quite,' says Nefarian.

'And now,' says Mal, 'let's eat.'

You take your place in his entourage, and Rostolph falls into step beside you.

'Good evening, sir,' he says.

'And to you, sir.'

'Nice to see our respective masters getting along so famously, is it not?'

'Indeed, it is not.'

'Ha ha! Very funny, Mr Artanon.'

You enter the castle and head to the dining hall. Carefully you remove Mal's ceremonial cloak and drape it over the back of his dragon bone chair. You ensure the sigils are on display and the feathers stick out nicely to either side.

'If you will excuse me, my lord?'

'Yes, yes, be off with you - I'm sure you have some food to organise!'

As you leave the hall, Rostolph once again materialises.

'Can I be of service, Mr Artanon?'

Turn to 184.

272

You enter Mrs Bleakheart's domain, a steamy washroom in which massive pots are stirred over open flames, cleaners restock their trolleys from mouldy supply cupboards, and maids strain on the handles of machines that squeeze moisture from sodden fabric.

Mrs Bleakheart herself stands in the midst of it all, sucking a stain out of a tablecloth. She is a stout orc in a white frock, whose life of lugging pots and crushing clothes has left her more muscular than many a soldier.

'Get those sheets on the boil,' she orders in a dry monotone. 'We've got I-don't-know-how-many rooms to make ready, each with a layer of dust for a bedspread. Hasn't been this many guests since his lordship was inaugurated, or I don't know about it.'

'Mrs Bleakheart.'

The housekeeper gives you a flat stare. 'Mr Artanon. I've a dozen tasks to do and a dozen moments to do 'em in, so whatever you want, I'll beg you keep it brief.'

Before you can respond, you hear a strange squeaking coming from a pot into which sheets are being loaded.

Do you want to investigate this noise?
Turn to 112.

Or do you take umbrage at your subordinate's attitude, no matter that she's served in the castle longer than you?
Turn to 8.

Perhaps you would like to suggest a better option for removing stains from cloth than orc spittle?
Turn to 150.

273

You linger outside the doorway, listening to the servant's chatter from within.
　'Poor Sarka,' someone says. 'Should we go and help her?'
　'Only if you want a clip around the ears,' comes Kalag's reply. 'Mr Artanon gave clear instruction to polish the tableware until you can see your own ugly face in it - and your reflection is still blurry enough to be mistaken for handsome. Let Sarka be, she'll only get hair all over everything anyway.'
　You are pleased to hear your second in command speak so firmly – it seems your faith in the young man is not misplaced.
　You decide to leave your staff to their work.

Turn to 211.

274

You sidle up besides Mal.

'... showed them what fear truly is, eh, lord?' a harpy nestmother crows. 'Burned those Brightlanders right out of their homes!'

'They were foolish to think they could stand against me,' says Mal.

Beside him, Captain Haiken nods dutifully, despite receiving none of the praise for the attack.

'Excuse me, Your Boastfulness,' you say quietly. 'If I might ...'

'Not now, Mr Artanon,' says Mal. 'Can't you see I'm busy regaling my loyal subjects with tales of my masochistic misdeeds?'

'It is a matter of some urgency, oh Vainglorious One ...'

Mal's hand turns to a fist. 'Mr Artanon, when I tell you to begone, begone!'

If he was not already, then MAL IS IRKED with you.

You glide away, wondering why you bother. From now on it is probably best to assume that Mal is too preoccupied, with the ceremony and all associated pomp, to deal sensibly with anything else. Even if you told him about what's afoot, he's just generally incapable of the delicate manoeuvrings necessary to ensure an optimal outcome.

You make up your mind to deal with the problem yourself, as any good butler would!

Turn to 142.

275

'Now you see here, Miss Molsk,' you say, putting on your sternest face, 'you get this place cleaned up spick and span, or I'll see to it that something very bad indeed happens to you.'

Molsk gets a funny grin on her cretinous face.

'That sounds like it would tickle, Mr Artanon.'

You really cannot believe this idiot has been left in charge for as long as she has.

You could still opt to shove her face into a mound of dung?
Turn to 107.

Or, if you have truly lost patience, why don't you reach beneath your robe for the dagger you keep about your person at all times, and stab her with it?
Turn to 93.

Or you could give up and leave?
Turn to 124.

276

'I am Mr Artanon,' you say, as you breathe in the smell of her smooth skin.

You have told Rose YOUR NAME.

What an honest fellow you are, Mr Artanon!

Turn to 258.

277

You make your way down, down, down to the cellar, deep in the belly of Cayfax Mountain. At the end of a cobwebbed passageway you come to an oaken door, outside of which stand two guards - for there are bottles within worth more than their weight in onyx.

'Evening, gentlemen.'

You unlock the door and enter a long dark room full of aisles of wine racks, in which the air is kept dry and cool by an enchanted box set on the wall called a 'conditioner of the air'.

You collect up some likely vintages. Perhaps you should taste-test them? Just to make sure they are high enough quality for the ceremony, of course? Or you could make your choices based on your excellent previous knowledge, without opening any bottles?

Will you try:

The *Graveyard Pearl* Black Sauvignon?
Turn to 197.

The Sparkling *Bloodworm's Rest* Cabernet?
Turn to 111.

Nargletarg's Vineyard Dry Blue?
Turn to 224.

Glasscandle's Premium Scorpion Whisky?
Turn to 14.

Mrs Plugberry's Make-Me-Feel-Nice Cure-All Tonic and Tile Cleaner?
Turn to 87.

Or, if you trust yourself to make excellent choices, pile up a cart full of booze and get out of here.
Turn to 168.

278

'Oh Heartless One!' you implore. 'Can you not forgive this one transgression from a loyal servant of many years? I promise that ...'

'Silence,' says Mal, and your mouth snaps shut involuntarily, breaking several of your teeth. For a moment Mal just stares at you, an unreadable expression on his face.

'Mr Artanon,' he says finally, shaking his head. 'I never would have guessed it. She must have done something truly obscene in order to tempt such a serious fellow.' He looks down at Roseblossom. 'I must say, girl, I admire your cunning. And your willingness to reap revenge. I have to wonder if perhaps you were born in the wrong land?'

'My lord?'

'I see now why Captain Haiken warned me off visiting you in the dungeon. You are very beautiful. No wonder you managed to tempt my wretched manservant.'

'Thank you.'

The weight across your shoulders grows heavier, but you cannot cry out through your welded-shut jaw. Your face pushes down into the grass.

'Perhaps,' says Mal, 'as an alternative to death, you would like to join my harem?'

The weight breaks your back.

Your service ends here.

279

You tap your foot impatiently as Repugnis puts together a platter of cheese, then head upstairs to the throne room.

Turn to 80.

280

'On second thoughts,' you say, 'perhaps I can come up with a better solution.'

'Very well,' says Jhurgle. 'So, was there something else?'

Turn to 253.

281

Luckily you had the forethought to dress appropriately for the occasion, and suffer no problems traversing the wall.

You reach the bottom and steal down the mountain slope, away from the main road to Cayfax Town. With any luck, it will hours before your escape route is detected. Still, it would be prudent to be swift!

As dawn begins to break, you find yourself leagues from the castle on stolen horses, galloping towards the border realms.

Turn to 296.

282

You step forward and clear your throat.

'Excuse my wheedlesome interruption, Your Frugalness,' you say, 'but I feel I must draw your attention to the priceless tapestry which this wretch currently cowers before. It would be an awful shame if it were devalued – by fireball, for example.'

Mal frowns at the tapestry in question. It depicts

his predecessor, Lord Varyon, standing atop a mound of slain Brightlanders, looking very pleased with himself.

'I always hated that tapestry anyway,' says Mal, flames collecting in his palm.

Turn to 71.

283

You enter Bojanda's workroom to find the harpy tailor standing before Mal's ceremonial robe, biting at the ends of her claws.

'Miss Bojanda?'

'Oh! Mr Artanon. I didn't hear you come in. Would you mind casting your eye over this garment for me, please? I've been staring at it long enough to lose objectivity.'

You do as she asks and size up the robe. It shines glossy black with nary a speck nor fluffball besmirching it. Gold threaded symbols of the Shadow God adorn the chest and sleeves, and assorted feathers spray from the shoulders.

'I think you've done an excellent job, Miss Bojanda.'

'You don't think the Sign of the Raven is a bit much? You know the old saying – put too much on then take something off?'

'I don't think Stygias will mind a nod towards his earthly spies. Honestly, Miss Bojanda, you should be proud.'

'Thank you, Mr Artanon. You have put my mind at ease. I will deliver it personally to His Stylishness's chambers.'

'Very good, ma'am.'

Next, will you check in with Mrs Bleakheart, the head housekeeper, to ensure that all is ready for the final round of guests arriving today?
Turn to 16.

Or round up any idle hands to polish the castle's best tableware for the feast?
Turn to 176.

Or go to your office?
Turn to 211.

284

The skull in the sky opens its mouth and sends forth a horrible groaning wind that blasts the clearing, flattening the grass. The sound vibrates in your ears, and you throw your hands up to cover them, lest your eardrums explode. The strength of it forces you to your knees, and with it comes a foul scent like a thousand corpses rotting in the mire – the ancient breath of Stygias himself.

'You dare,' thunders his unearthly voice, 'insult the God of Shadows?'

'My lord!' Mal screams, flinging himself prostate. 'I beg you, let me right this wrong! We can start the ceremony again ...'

Blood seeps down the moon's yellow face, bathing everything in a red glow.

'You have failed me,' booms Stygias, 'and so you must be punished.'

'Lord! No! Please, let me ...'

Mal's words are cut off as he shrieks in agony.

You can understand his problem. All around you people writhe in torment and scrabble at the grass.

The ringing in your ears increases to a torturous thrum, until you feel blood burst from your eyes. A moment later your skull shatters inside your head.
'Your souls in payment,' comes Stygias's voice. Your service ends here.

285

Go on, Mr Artanon, what could be the harm? It's not every day you get a chance to look upon a young sacrifice to the God of Shadows, may his claws rake furrows in the world? What do you say?

'Well, all right then.'
Turn to 104.

'I already made this choice, damn it, now let me drop this wine off in the kitchen and get to my bed!'
Turn to 96.

286

As the chanting grows louder, you hear an unearthly baying off in the woods. Given the general atmosphere, no one really bats an eye.
An answering howl goes up near the first, and two wolfish voices combine into a deranged ululation. Their owners bound off together, and the sound fades into the night.
It seems that Feralis and Sarka have met under the light of the full moon, and are working off their bestial urges.
You are satisfied that you have avoided a potential problem.

Turn to 42.

287

As the globe hits the bottom of the bin, it smashes.
'Bet you didn't see that coming,' you say, with a sneer.
Very droll, Mr Artanon.
Back to your letters and whatnot, sir.

Turn to 92.

288

'Hmm,' you say to yourself. 'Hmmmmm.'
Where will you find a passable substitute, Mr Artanon?
Jars of powder make you think of the spice cupboard in the kitchen. Looking like you're on a mission (which you are), you enter the kitchen and go to the cupboard. Shelves of exotic spices crowd your vision, and you scan for something similar to the red dust you saw. One jar stands out over the others, and you inspect the label.
'Paprika.'
Perfect.
You are a PAPRIKA SMUGGLER.

Turn to 235.

289

'I think it is time we return to our duties,' you respond. 'Repugnis has enough on his plate without having to serve servants - don't you, Repugnis?'
'Yes, Mr Artanon.'

'A shame!' says Rostolph. 'But never mind. I shall resolve to hope for leftovers once the feast is done.'

'You do that, sir.'

Rostolph leaves the kitchen, and you watch him go with a growing distrust. Still, distrust is everywhere, so perhaps it is nothing special.

Speaking of distrust, it's probably time you checked in at your office.

Turn to 142.

290

Roseblossom's sorrow turns to rage, and she slaps you hard across the face – something you undoubtedly deserve.

You push her away and leave the cell, locking the door behind you.

'May you burn in the sunshine of the afterlife!' she screams. 'May celestial buzzards rip your kidneys out every day!'

'Your Gods have no power here, my dove,' you mutter as you walk away - but it's not an entirely comforting thought. Your own Gods are hardly going to be ecstatic with what you have done.

It will truly be a wonder if you survive this mistake, Mr Artanon.

For now, deliver the booze to the kitchen before it causes you any more trouble, then think about how you might rectify this situation on your way to bed.

Turn to 96.

291

'Sarka!' you snap, making her start. She gets to her feet, snuffles and wipes her wet snout with the back of her paw.

'Have you no sense of decorum?' you ask. 'The castle is full of honoured guests. Do you think they want to see you acting all hangdog in the corner?'

'My apologies, Mr Artanon.'

'What's the matter?'

'Nothing, sir.'

'Tell me what has caused this breach of propriety or I will breach your arse with my boot.'

Sarka stiffens. 'They were talking in the kitchen, sir, about how Mr Rostolph's brother was just recently executed by his Lordship Nefarian. Remarking that it must be difficult for a servant to maintain loyalty in such circumstances.'

If you did not already, you now know about ROSTOLPH'S BROTHER.

'And why has that led to you encrusting the corridors in salt?'

'It's just that my own brother died recently, sir, of heartworm. I was reminded of it, and it made me sad.'

'Well,' you say, 'while I find this display of sentimentality extremely touching, something else in need of touching is the tableware for this evening. You will have further reason to be sad if you do not immediately return to work.'

'Yessir, Mr Artanon, sir.'

Sarka ducks her head, and makes off in the direction of the common room.

Turn to 211.

292 – The End

'Where ...' chokes Nefarian, clutching Rostolph's arm, 'did you put ... the poison?'

'Into the peas, lord, like we planned.'

'You ... liar!'

Rostolph cries out as an invisible force hurls him off his feet against the wall, where his head smashes upon the stone.

Normally such an incident would gain attention, but everywhere nobles are rising from their seats to splutter and convulse with eyes full of panic.

'What ... is ... the meaning of ... erk ...'

'My heart – it's going to explode!'

'Save us, Lord Malacandros!'

Mal, however, is having his own problems. His veins have turned black and stand out against his skin. His face is distorted by pain, and a moment later he pitches forward onto the table. He twitches there, white foam building at the corners of his mouth, until he lies still.

Around the chamber the same thing is happening to all of the nobles. Some try to run, but don't make it far before agony cripples them. Plates are knocked to the floor and fingernails rake down tapestries.

'Mr Artanon!' Kalag arrives at your side, his eyes wide. 'What's happening, sir? What should we do?'

'I'm afraid there isn't much we can do,' you say, as you watch Nocturnia's elite collapse into a writhing, frothy pile. The poison is apparently swift-acting and merciless – it takes a savagely short time for the screaming to die down.

Servants stand stunned amidst the ruin, while others who enter gasp and drop their trays.

'Dispose of the feast!' you bark, making them all snap to attention. 'Something in the food was bad!

292 (cont'd)

Get rid of it all before anyone else suffers!'

Seemingly grateful for the order, the staff swing into action. Meanwhile Captain Erkenslaw rushes from body to body, but finds no survivors.

'Mr Artanon! It's a tragedy! The entire nobility of Nocturnia is dead!'

'Well now, dear sir, I wouldn't say that. There are a scattering of ladies and lordlings not currently in attendance. That said, anyone not present must be treated as suspect of committing this terrible crime. After all, who else stands to benefit?'

Erkenslaw frowns. 'Indeed, Mr Artanon. Only someone who sought to clear the way to the top job would engineer this travesty.'

'Someone so far down the ladder that almost everyone else would have to wiped out for them to even stand a chance.'

'Damn them!' Erkenslaw punches his fist. 'Whoever they are, they must not be allowed to triumph. The throne must not be given over to such a reckless contender.'

'I agree. In the meantime, it is up to us to keep the castle well maintained and protected, for whoever might rightfully rise.'

Erkenslaw nods earnestly. 'Yes, yes – you are wise, Mr Artanon. What should we do first?'

'I think clearing away the dead would be a good start, Captain.'

Erkenslaw salutes you and goes to supervise his guards.

You cannot help but notice that everyone is deferring to you. A natural thing, perhaps – after all, your authority over the castle staff was second only to Malacandros. With him gone, well ... it's almost as if *you're* the Dark Lord now.

Eh, Mr Artanon?

293 – The End

Everybody eats and laughs and spills food down their fronts, sometimes all at the same time. Servants move in an endless train, clearing tables and bringing fresh plates. All is very jolly and well. The exceptions are Nefarian and Rostolph, who you observe glancing from Mal's peas to Mal – first with an air of anticipation, then growing confusion, and finally, as Mal fails to have any reaction to the peas other than to call them his tasty green darlings, consternation. It seems that perhaps they were expecting something to happen which has not come to pass. Consequently, they are rather discombobulated. Forced to forget any declarations of triumph he might have had planned, Nefarian resorts to forcing smiles as various nobles engage him in conversation.

'More eel terrine, my lord?' you ask, bending over his shoulder to cut him a slice.

'Ah ... yes, thank you, Mr Artanon.'

You serve him and step back next to Rostolph.

'I can serve my own lord, thank you, Mr Artanon,' he says snippily.

You ignore the comment, choosing instead to gesture around at the celebration. 'What a success, eh, Mr Rostolph? Everything running smoothly, everyone having a bad old time, and no unforeseen complications.'

Rostolph regards you levelly.

'Why, Mr Rostolph, you look glummer than a man whose *nefarious* plot has somehow been thwarted.'

That really gets his attention.

'I can imagine,' you continue, 'that in such a circumstance, any potential perpetrators would be thankful for their enduring anonymity. They could always try their luck again in the future – at the next Stygias Ceremony, perhaps? It's only a century away, after all. In the meantime, they could always relax and enjoy themselves - it's not as if the fine folk gathered here are any the wiser to their foiled schemes.'

Rostolph stares at you for a long moment.

'Mr Rostolph?' you prompt.

Eventually, he sighs. 'I have always thought,' he says, 'that discretion was the better part of butlering.'

'I would have to agree.'

Rostolph nods with begrudging respect. 'I see now how you manage to keep the top job, Mr Artanon.'

It seems he knows when he's been out-buttled.

Well done, Mr Artanon. Everything has gone off without a hitch. The celebration rages into the wee hours, and all agree it is the best feast in a hundred years.

As for you, sir – you have been an excellent butler to the Dark Lord.

294 – The End

You're a funny one, aren't you, Mr Artanon? You learned of Nefarian's dastardly plan, stole the poison and exchanged it for paprika, then went ahead and poisoned Malacandros anyway. And since you followed their original scheme, Nefarian and Rostolph think it was all their own doing. So why did you kill Mal? For personal reasons? Did you just want the satisfaction of knowing it was you who truly ended his life?

The Dark Lord truly must have irked you.

Stygias knows what will happen to you now. No one thinks they owe you anything, and with Nefarian in power, and no doubt bringing his personal staff with him, it's doubtful you'll be asked to carry on in your current capacity. In fact you'll be lucky not to get fired – after all, it's not like you're a very good butler, is it? You poisoned your master for no real benefit.

Maybe it's time to slip away, and fetch that bottle of antique wine from the cellar which no one else knows about – remember, the one worth a fortune? You might be able to sell it to a collector for enough onyx to ensure your financial survival. That's if you don't get reckless and just drink it in the meantime, which frankly sounds like the kind of thing someone like you might do.

Well, you have to live, eh?

On your way then, Mr Artanon.

295 – The End

Well, Mr Artanon, this is most unfortunate. You have failed to notice anything which would have allowed you to save your employer, or alternatively, align yourself with his competitors. A good butler should know everything that is going on under his roof, yet it seems that you have not been paying attention.

At least the cutlery was clean. Still, you cannot help but feel that you could have done more. That you could have been a bit less, now let's see, what's the word? Ah yes. 'Useless'.

As celebration of the new Dark Lord breaks into full swing around you, Rostolph sidles up to you gleefully.

'Hello, Mr Artanon. Now that I am butler to the

Dark Lord, we will have to find a new position for you in the household hierarchy. Candlestick cleaner, perhaps? Or latrine hygiene specialist? But never fear – if you work hard every day, who knows? Eventually you might get promoted all the way back up to third footman.'

You resist the urge to invert his nose into his face. In the current climate, such an act would see you quickly follow your master into the afterlife.

'That is,' says Rostolph, 'unless you wish to turn in your notice? I hear there is plenty of work to be found in spider farming right now.'

Well, Mr Artanon, whatever you choose to do from here on in, it's really up to you. Be assured, however, that no one cares.

Have a nice life, Mr Artanon.

296 – The End

You have successfully escaped from Cayfax Castle with Roseblossom!

You push the horses for days, staying off-road and out of sight. Eventually you find an abandoned hut by a forest and a babbling brook, where Roseblossom begs you to rest a while. The question of what to do next is a difficult one – as a Brightlander and a Nocturnian, there is no place in the world where you both are welcome.

Days pass, and you come to realise that Rose is pregnant – undoubtedly with some half-caste mongrel who will lead a miserable life as an outcast, if he even survives. As you try to think of what to do next, you absent-mindedly take to patching up the hut and collecting spiders from the wood. You could always start farming them again, couldn't you?

And while, in certain lights, to some perceptions, you have made the right moral choice by saving the damsel in distress, that really wasn't the point, was it? Such heroism just doesn't seem 'in character' for a fellow like yourself. Perhaps this would be considered a happy ending in certain other stories, but for you it means a life lived in exile, and a bastard child who serves as an ongoing reminder that you have utterly failed to do your duty.

Hope you're satisfied, Mr Artanon. You weren't really a very good butler to the Dark Lord, were you?

297 – The End

As Mal's body is dragged from the dining hall by his former guards, you busy yourself stacking up empty plates in a bid to be gone from the room. As you retreat down a corridor, however, a familiar voice halts you.

'Mr Artanon.'

You turn to find Rostolph smiling at you.

'Mr Rostolph.'

'My lord has not forgotten your part in our little power play.'

He tosses you a cloth bag. Deftly, you catch it on a dirty plate with a clink.

It is quite heavy. Really quite heavy.

'Please give him my thanks,' you say. 'And to you also, Mr Rostolph.'

'Unfortunately,' continues Rostolph, 'now that he is Dark Lord, Nefarian will, of course, retain me as his butler. I'm sure we can find some other position to befit you, of course ... first footman, for example?'

Rostolph's words instantly appal you. You cannot imagine taking orders from this ratty little upstart.

'Or I could enquire,' he goes on, 'as to whether a butlering position is available in one of the other noble houses?'

You are always across such things, and would have heard if anyone important was looking for such a person.

'First footman will suit me well, thank you, sir,' you say. 'I prefer to serve the Dark Lord himself, even if less directly than before. Cayfax Castle is my home.'

Rostolph nods. 'As you wish. Please hand me your master key, sir.'

Again comes a coldness in your belly, and again you squash it down - for now. You pull out your key and hand it to Rostolph. As you do, you make yourself a promise that you will not rest until this bald piece of shit is shamed, discharged, or better yet, dead. You don't think it will take you very long – you know the castle inside and out, and all who dwell within it. You have the practice, too. Getting rid of those above is how you became butler to the Dark Lord in the first place.

'You are very kind to keep me on,' you say. 'I look forward to continuing my service under new management.'

It will simply depend on what choices you make, won't it, Mr Artanon?

Have fun.

298 – The End

'Yes,' you announce, stepping forward, 'it is poison, my lord. Nefarian and his man Rostolph enlisted me to help murder you, yet I put the poison into Nefarian's food instead.'

298 (cont'd)

'Mr Artanon!' exclaims Mal. 'Why didn't you tell me about this?'

'I did not want to ruin your special day,' you say.

Nefarian's eyes blaze with rage. Rostolph screams and runs at you, a dagger emerging from beneath his clothes. Mal shoots out a hand and Rostolph flies backwards off his feet, to hit some ceremonial weapons on the wall, which impale him rather unceremoniously.

'You ... will ... die ... with ... me,' manages Nefarian, through flecks of froth.

'I know,' you say.

'What is he talking about, Mr Artanon?' asks Mal.

'He bonded my heart to his,' you reply. 'When he dies, so shall I.'

Mal frowns. 'That old chestnut.'

Nefarian slides to the floor where he begins to spasm. You do not feel the pain yourself, thankfully – it is apparently not that kind of voodoo. However, the moment that Nefarian gasps his last gasp, death for you is instant.

Mal gives a surprisingly sentimental cry, and leaps to seize you by the shoulders. It is too late. Slowly, you collapse to the floor with blank eyes.

'Mr Artanon!' says Mal. 'I will see that your family is rewarded for your loyalty!'

You do not hear him. A strange, dark tunnel opens up beneath you, and sucks your soul downwards. Beside you, you notice something swirl, and look over to see Nefarian's ephemeral spirit staring at you with hatred.

'Stygias curse your soul!' he hisses.

'I do not think so, lord,' you reply. 'I saved his chosen Dark Lord from an untimely demise, after all. You, on the other hand, I don't imagine he will be so happy with.'

Nefarian's eyes fill with the horror of this realisation.

Perhaps someone will need a good butler in the afterlife? And something tells you your references will be good.

This result has come at some cost – but well done, Mr Artanon.

299 – The End

'Lord Bentle,' says Rostolph, turning to a fat fellow who was one of Nefarian's closest allies. 'You know I was a close and respected advisor to Lord Nefarian – that he treated me better than any servant has a right to be!'

Bentle shifts uncomfortably in his seat, but finds his voice nonetheless. 'It's true,' he says. 'I know no reason why this butler would murder his own benefactor.'

'The facts speak for themselves,' you interject. 'I saw Mr Rostolph through a keyhole to his quarters, experimenting with a jar of poison.'

'What keen powers of observation,' Rostolph sneers, 'to behold the properties of distant jars through keyholes, Mr Artanon. How do you know it was poison, sir? Maybe it was a jar of spice? Or facial ointment? My poor master did suffer from the occasional blemish, Stygias rest his soul.'

You open your mouth to respond but Rostolph quickly cuts you off.

'I believe it was you,' Rostolph jabs a finger, 'who served my lord his last slice of eel terrine, was it not? Did anyone else notice?' He sends the question in the direction of nobles closest to Nefarian's body.

'I did see that, actually,' says one.

299 (cont'd)

'Me too.'

'Mmm, yes.'

You are beginning to feel that this isn't going very well.

'Mr Artanon, is this true?' asks Mal. He does not look about to rise to your defence. He looks like a Dark Lord eager to maintain the loyalty of his subjects.

'I did not serve him the first slice,' you say levelly. 'He did that for himself.'

'And who was it asked me just the other day,' says Rostolph, 'what my lord's favourite dish was? And who had a hand in setting the table so whatever dish they'd poisoned would be close to him?'

'How dare you murder my honoured guests, Mr Artanon,' says Mal, summoning a display of righteous anger. 'That is not very good butlering, I must declare.'

Oh well. You saved the day, Mr Artanon – or rather, you saved a selfish Dark Lord who would rather see you dead than thank you for his life. Your commitment to professionalism has been second to none, but unfortunately, as with all good butlers, your best work has gone unnoticed. This is how it should be, and you never expected any great fanfare for doing your job - but you also did not expect to be burned alive by magical fire for your trouble.

Perhaps, you think, as flames crackle the fat beneath your skin, Stygias will have need of an excellent butler in the afterlife?

As far as this one goes, however, your service is at an end.

300 – The End

You allow a tight smile to flit across your mouth.

'Mr Artanon?' says Mal. 'Come, if you have some insight ...'

'Only,' you say, 'that if one was looking for motive to attach to Mr Rostolph's actions, one would have to look no further then the fact ...' You pause for dramatic effect. '... that Lord Nefarian killed his brother!'

This causes a stir along the table.

'Yes, I heard about that ...'

'Mm, my serving girl told me the gossip ...'

'Is this true?' Mal asks Rostolph, his cold voice silencing the chatter.

'My lord,' Rostolph says desperately, 'I swear, I had no love for my brother at all. He was an embarrassment to my family! When he dropped a stack of dishes for the third time in a month, it was *I* who counselled Nefarian to have him ...'

'Ah, the family bond!' you interject. 'Is there anything stronger? Even when we fight amongst our own kin, we appreciate the importance of sticking together. You would understand that, of course, oh Grieving One? For even though you and Lord Nefarian were not the closest of cousins, you are nevertheless horrified by his death!'

Mal takes a moment to cotton on. 'What? Oh! Yes, of course. Quite horrified.'

'Then what wrath you must feel towards his killer, Your Vengefulness!'

Mal's eyes narrow on Rostolph. 'Indeed.'

'No!' yelps Rostolph, spreading his hands. 'Please listen, my lord ...'

'How dare you poison my beloved cousin!'

'My lord, I entreat you ...'

300 (cont'd)

Twisting vines issue up from the floor to wrap around Rostolph and raise him towards the ceiling. They encircle his neck, cutting off his objections and making his eyes bulge. He manages to find your gaze, though he is too constricted to project any expression other than 'suffocating'. You gaze back impassively.

'You will pay,' shouts Mal, 'for the sorrow you have caused!'

The vines stretch out, pulling on Rostolph's limbs. He tries to scream, but has no air for it. A moment later his arms tear from their sockets, legs from his hips, and his head thumps down into the empty balfrog tureen.

The nobles glance around, unsure how to react.

'Oh, Stygias,' Mal says, burying his face in his palms. 'Please grant safe passage to my cousin's soul as he journeys into the afterlife. Please ...'

He does a remarkably bad job of pretending to weep.

A young noblewoman rises, clutching her hand to her breast. 'My lord,' she says earnestly, 'allow me to offer my heartfelt sympathies ...'

This idea spreads incredibly quickly, and others scramble to add their voices to a growing chorus of condolence.

'Just give me a moment, dear friends,' says Mal. 'I must recover myself.' He turns away from the gathering, as if wracked by misery. Surreptitiously, he beckons you over.

'Think you can get the dining hall cleaned up in time for dessert, Mr Artanon?'

'Of course, my lord.'

'Snap to it, then.'

You bow, and are about to leave.

'Oh,' adds Mal, 'and Mr Artanon?'

'Yes, oh Disingenuous One?'

'I think it's about time you received a raise, don't you?'

You cock an eyebrow. 'I believe that may well be the case, my lord.'

'Very well. And now,' he raises his voice for the benefit of all, 'get this room cleared of painful memories before I burn the skin right off your body!'

You bow again, and get to work.

What an excellent butler you are, Mr Artanon.

Also by Sam Bowring

PROPHECY'S RUIN
Book 1 of the Broken Well trilogy

For a millennium the lands of Kainordas and Fenvarrow have been at war, ever since the gods of shadow and light broke the Great Well of Souls. In the absence of victory a stalemate persists – until a prophecy foretells of a child of power who will destroy the balance forever. Mages from the two lands race to claim the newborn, but in a ferocious battle of magic fought over the baby, his very soul is ripped apart, leaving two boys in its wake. Each side seizes a child, uncertain whether they now possess the one capable of victory.

Starring psychopathic goblins, undead mages, indestructible butterflies, shape-shifting swamp monsters and an evil talking bird.

'If you are sick of cliché heroes and villains then this is the one to read'
– Australian Bookseller + Publisher

BLACK MARKET PRAWNS
Episode 1 of Sam, Jake and Dylan Want Money

Sam, Jake and Dylan are three degenerate losers who live on the 42nd floor of Hazy Towers, the worst apartment block in the known universe. They don't have jobs, or buy food, or ever pay a single cent of rent to their spineless landlord, Mr Hayes, because it's so much cheaper just to slam the door in his pitiful face. Still, government handouts only buy so much booze, and the boys are always looking for a crazy way to make a buck.

Grab Episode 1 for free online.

Printed in Great Britain
by Amazon